"Well, hi, Mrs Morgan," Jed said softly, caressing her wedding band.

Jed continued, "How about a 'Welcome home' kiss for the injured warrior?"

Sarah's lips parted in a gasp.

Her eyes sparked with indignation.

Jed did a mental double-take. Had they quarreled, before his accident? He leaned forward and claimed her parted pink lips with his own.

Grace Green grew up in Scotland but later emigrated to Canada with her husband and children. They settled in 'Beautiful Super Natural BC' and Grace now lives in a house just minutes from ocean, beaches, mountains and rainforest. She makes no secret of her favourite occupation—her bumper sticker reads: I'D RATHER BE WRITING ROMANCE! Grace also enjoys walking the sea wall, gardening, getting together with other authors...and watching her characters come to life, because she knows that once they do they will take over and write her stories for her.

Recent titles by the same author:

THE FATHERHOOD SECRET

A HUSBAND WORTH WAITING FOR

BY
GRACE GREEN

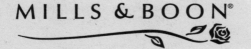

MILLS & BOON®

For John

First published in Great Britain 1999
Harlequin Mills & Boon Limited,
Eton House, 18-24 Paradise Road, Richmond, Surrey TW9 1SR

© Grace Green 1999

ISBN 0 263 81938 8

Set in Times Roman 10½ on 12 pt.
02-0002-44700 C1

Printed and bound in Spain
by Litografía Rosés, S.A., Barcelona

CHAPTER ONE

WHERE on *earth* was Jedidiah Morgan?

Sarah shivered in the bone-chilling rain as she banged the wolf-head door knocker for the umpteenth time. She'd come all this way to throw herself on the man's mercy—he just *had* to be at home!

"Mom—" Emma's voice was plaintive "—I'm hungry."

Sarah glanced wearily at the six-year-old sagging against her on the lamp-lit stoop. Rain streamed down Emma's yellow slicker; ran down her wistful, up-turned face.

"Honey, I'm sure your uncle will have a big fridge packed with food, if this fine house is anything to go by." She'd carried three-year-old Jamie from the car and now, as her left shoulder cramped, she shifted his weight.

Stirring, he murmured, "Mommie, I wanna go bed."

Sarah cuddled him closer. "Soon, sweetie. Soon."

She wanted to go to bed, too. She'd driven over three hundred miles since leaving Quesnel and for the last seventy the foul weather had reduced visibility to almost nil. The drive up Whispering Mountain to Morgan's Hope had been a nightmare; the stress of it had left her totally drained.

She squeezed back a welling of tears. What a mess she'd made of things. And what a fool she'd been to make this trip, using up precious dollars for gas on what was turning out to be nothing more than a wild-goose chase.

Turning, she looked despairingly into the pitch-black night.

The storm wasn't letting up—if anything, it was becoming even more savage. She flinched as lightning flashed across the sky. For a fleeting moment, the zig-zagging strobe lit up the wide graveled sweep, her rusted blue Cutlass, the surrounding forest of ever-greens—

"Mom!" Emma's eager voice reached her over the rising gale. "The door's not locked!"

Sarah swiveled around.

Emma had opened the door a crack.

"Honey!" Sarah shot an arm out to stop her. "Don't—"

Too late. Emma had swung the door inward and had already moved forward into the shadowy en-tranceway.

Sarah hesitated. Then with a grimace, she stepped nervously after her daughter, jumping as a draft caught the door and slammed it shut behind them.

In the glow through the fanlight from the lamp out-side, she saw a switch on the wall. Heart thudding, she flicked it on.

Emma was already walking ahead into a large foyer decorated with sleek, pale oak furniture and graced by an elegant curving staircase. Rain dripped from her daughter's slicker, leaving a trail of dime-size stains on the taupe Berber carpet.

"Wait!" Sarah called softly.

"Let's find the kitchen, Mom."

Sarah glanced at Jamie and saw he'd fallen asleep. She bit her lip undecidedly. She knew she ought to go over to the staircase and shout, 'Helloooo?' But if she did, she'd waken Jamie. Besides, it was *obvious* nobody was at home; she'd hammered the door loudly enough to waken the dead.

And the house had that unmistakably 'empty' feel to it.

Emma sat down and tugged off her pink rubber boots. Scrambling to her feet, she tossed her wet slicker on top of the boots and padded determinedly along a corridor to the left that led to the back of the house.

Sarah expelled a wry sigh. From the moment Emma Jane Morgan had drawn her first breath, she'd gone doggedly after what she wanted and tonight was apparently to be no exception!

Following in her wake, Sarah flicked on another light, revealing an open doorway at the far end of the corridor.

"It's down here, Mom!" Entering the room, Emma rose on her tiptoes and had just hit the light switch when her mother caught up with her.

If Sarah hadn't been so tired, she knew she'd have drooled over this kitchen. It could have been lifted straight off the glossy cover of *Fabulous Homes*.

Black. White. And chrome. Everything sparkling, spotless and dazzling. From the white-tiled floor, to the granite countertops, to the state-of-the-art appliances.

The recessed dining area was furnished with black leather–cushioned banquettes and a granite-topped table, while sleek white miniblinds on windows and patio door closed out all sight of the storm raging outside.

The shiny black fridge was zero clearance.

And Emma had already opened the door.

The child's gaze widened as she stared inside. ''Mom!'' Her voice cracked. ''You were right. It's loaded!''

Sarah unwrapped Jamie from his slicker and settled him on one of the banquettes before moving to join Emma.

The fridge was, indeed, 'loaded.'

Sarah's stomach felt hollow with hunger and the knowledge that Emma's probably felt the same squashed her qualms as she rummaged among cheeses and packaged meats, cartons of milk and bottles of orange juice.

She found a bowl of homemade soup, rich with carrots and tomatoes and rice. In a chrome bread bin, she found a whole-wheat loaf.

Minutes later, she and Emma were seated at the table, the homey smell of toast and savory soup filling the kitchen as they tucked in voraciously.

''What time is it, Mom?'' Emma talked in a whisper to avoid waking Jamie.

''Almost midnight!''

''Holy moly!'' Gray eyes round as saucers, Emma asked, ''Have I ever been up this late before?''

''Not that I recall.'' Sarah's gaze flitted to a calendar on the wall just above Emma's head. It was bare of notations except for one on the last square of the month, where someone had hand-printed: MINERVA LEAVING.

"Mom, what are we going to do after we've eaten?"

Sarah directed her attention back to Emma. "We'll find a room with a sofa—armchairs—somewhere we can sleep."

"Can't we sleep in a bed?"

"No. Your uncle might not like that. But I'll go upstairs and look for some blankets so we can be cozy."

"How come Daddy never brought us here?"

"I don't know, honey." Which was, and was not, the truth. She knew that Chance had kept away from Morgan's Hope because he and his brother were estranged, but she had no idea what had caused the estrangement because Chance had always refused to discuss it.

"Where *is* our uncle?" Emma tugged free a strand of rain-damp hair that was stuck to her cheek.

"He can't be far away." The front door had, after all, been unlocked. Although that could have been an oversight. The man could be in Timbuktu! But no, if he'd gone on a trip, he'd have gotten rid of the perishables in his fridge.

Emma licked the last drops of soup from her spoon. "Maybe he went for a walk."

"I shouldn't think so. Not in this storm."

But if he hadn't gone for a walk, reflected Sarah—and it would be crazy to think he had!—then where in the world *was* Jedidiah Morgan?

Jedidiah Morgan swept his palm smoothly across the woman's alabaster-white shoulders. Running a caressing fingertip over her collarbone, he let it linger in the valley between her breasts. And then, eyes narrowed, he scrutinized the breasts themselves. Tilting his head, he examined the voluptuous curves before moving his gaze to the peaks.

An ironic smile played around his mouth as he flicked an erect nipple with his thumb pad.

"Perfect," he said.

And finished. At last.

He stretched, yawned, and squinted at his watch.

Midnight.

He'd lost all sense of time. It was always the same when his work was going well.

"Hey, Max." He whistled to the black Lab snoozing on the mat by the woodstove. "Time to go."

The dog lifted his head, fixed his golden-brown eyes on his master. Then he stretched, yawned and pushed himself up. Black tail wagging, he trotted to the studio door.

Jed could hear the rain drumming on the roof as it had been doing all day. Shrugging on his anorak, he scooped up his heavy-duty flashlight from the bench.

When he stepped outside, needles of rain spiked his face. Ducking his head, he made for the path through the forest. Max snuffled away into the bushes. He'd catch up soon enough, Jed reflected as he played the beam of the flashlight ahead to light his way over the muddy path. And sure enough, by the time he got to the house a few minutes later, Max was panting impatiently on the front stoop.

"Right, boy." Jed opened the door. "Snack and then bed." He flicked on the foyer light…and froze as a couple of things hit him like a punch on the jaw.

First…the sight of dark, wet tracks on his carpet.

Second…the smell of toast from his kitchen.

Max growled.

"Quiet!" Jed snapped his fingers. "Sit!"

The dog sat.

With soundless steps, Jedidiah headed along the shadowy corridor to the kitchen. Ahead, the kitchen door was ajar; the room in darkness.

He halted just outside the doorway and listened. He heard nothing but the faint hum of the fridge. The room had that 'empty' feel to it.

Nerves jumping nevertheless, he snapped on the light.

Everything looked as it had when he'd left.

He opened the fridge door. And was about to close it when he noticed that yesterday's leftover soup was gone.

Frowning, he opened the dishwasher.

The soup bowl was in the lower rack. Along with two soup plates and two side plates. Two spoons and a knife were slotted in the cutlery rack.

Adrenaline rushed through his veins. Someone had been here. Had eaten in his kitchen—

From the foyer came the sound of Max growling. A low, menacing sound, deep in the animal's throat, a growl that stirred the hair at Jed's nape.

He headed back along the corridor, keeping close to the wall.

Max was in his line of sight.

The intruder was not.

The Lab's hackles were up, and he was staring at somebody Jed couldn't see. Max's fangs gleamed white as he pulled his mouth back in a hostile snarl.

Warily, Jed edged forward, inch by inch, till he could peek around the corner—

The intruder was a woman. And one he had never seen before.

His astonished gaze flicked over her. Young and attractive, the stranger had a petite figure swamped in an oversize white shirt that billowed out over a pair of jeans. Her hair was honey-blond and long. Her face was heart-shaped and white. Her eyes were dark-lashed and gray.

And those dark-lashed gray eyes were fixed, with a wide look of terror, on Max.

Max was glaring, equally intensely, at her.

She took a cautious half step forward. Max growled.

She swiftly stepped back. Max barked.

She looked as if she was about to start crying.

Jed muttered, ''Damn!'' and walked into the foyer.

When she saw him, she almost jumped out of her skin. Good grief, he thought, she's a bag of nerves. But what the *hell* was she doing in his house?

''Max, shut up!'' He signaled and the dog slunk over. ''Kitchen!''

The Lab departed. With obvious reluctance.

Jed turned again to the stranger and felt a jolt of alarm when he saw that her face had gone from deathly white to a sickly green. She was staring at him as if he were a specter. For the first time he noticed the purple shadows smudging the skin under her eyes—eyes that had taken on the glazed expression of somebody in deep shock.

Was she going to pass out? He poised to move and catch her if it became necessary.

She pressed the fingertips of her left hand to her throat. He saw she was wearing a plain gold band on her ring finger.

"I'm sorry." Her voice came out in a raw whisper. "It's just that...I thought for a moment..."

He glowered at her. "Thought what?"

"I thought—" she cleared her throat of its huskiness "—I thought...for a second...that you were... Chance."

Chance? Now Jed was the one who was shocked. Shocked and utterly confused. What did this woman want? And why was she standing, in his house, talking about the one person in the world he hated with an obsession that bordered on insanity?

"Who the *hell* are *you*?" He clenched his hands into fists...and saw her flinch.

Drawing in a sharp breath, she stared at him. "I'm Sarah." Her voice held a tremor. "Sarah Morgan."

"*Morgan*?"

"Your...sister-in-law."

"*Sister-in-law*?" He was beginning to sound like an imbecilic parrot.

"Yes." Her voice had steadied somewhat. "I'm Chance's wife—" she grimaced "—Chance's widow, I mean. I find it difficult to get used to saying that, after—"

"Chance is *dead*?"

"He died, in a car accident, seven months ago."

Sarah had never seen anyone lose color so quickly.

But even as she felt a surge of compassion for him, she struggled to regain her own equilibrium after the shock *she* had just received. It had never occurred to her that Chance and his brother would be so alike.

The hair was the same: coal-black, rich. The features were the same: lean, rugged. The eyes: green, deep set. The nose: ridged. The figure: tall, rangy...

The only difference she could see was one of attitude. Whereas Chance had had the con man's built-in charm, his older brother had a dark, brooding aura reminiscent of a character in some Gothic novel.

"You just turn up here, out of the blue, to tell me my brother's dead?" His tone was harsh with animosity. "Okay, you've told me." His black eyebrows beetled down over his hostile eyes. "So now you can go."

Good grief, the man was a Heathcliff clone! Sarah speared him with an incredulous glare. "You'd put us out in this storm?"

His lips thinned. "Ah, yes. Us. Two plates, two spoons. So...who did Goldilocks bring with her? A lover perhaps?"

Sarah's mouth fell open. She'd just told this man her husband was dead and he was accusing her of—oh, unbelievable! Her outrage almost choked her.

"Not a lover?" He raised the dark eyebrows cynically. "Then just...a friend?"

"No." She sent him a look as hostile as any of his own. "I have my *children* with me. Emma and Jamie. They're sleeping, at the moment, in your sitting room."

He looked at her for a long, stark moment, and then he laughed. It was not a pleasant sound. "So you've brought children with you. Chance's children, I presume?"

"Of course!" Anger sent blood racing to her cheeks. "Of course they're Chance's children!"

''Then you have even more nerve than I'd imagined, Mrs. Sarah Morgan.' His face had become completely devoid of emotion. ''Now if you'll tell me what you've *really* come for, we can get it over with and you can be on your way.''

Her expression must have told its own story.

His smile was grim. ''How did I know? Well, if you'd just wanted to tell me my brother was dead, a phone call—even a letter—would have done the trick. So, Mrs. Morgan, what is it that you want from me?''

She hated him. Didn't even know him but hated him already. ''I need money,'' she said in a frigid tone. ''When your brother died, I discovered he'd left a mountain of unpaid bills. I can't afford to pay them, and—''

''How cleverly put,'' he jeered. '''My brother.' Let me put that another way for you. Shall we call him…your husband?''

Hateful, despicable…malicious. ''All right,'' she retorted. ''My husband. But he *was* your brother.''

''So,'' he said. ''How much?''

It was a huge amount. She tried not to stumble over it.

He shrugged. ''Fine. When you get where you're going, send me the request in writing, and I'll courier you a certified cheque.''

''Thank you,'' she said stiffly. ''I appreciate—''

''If that's it—'' his tone was brusque ''—I'd like you to get in your car—I assume you came by car?''

''Yes, but—''

''I'd like you to take your children, and get in your car, and get off the mountain right now.''

Sarah tried not to wither under his glittering green

gaze. "The children are exhausted. Could we possibly stay here, just for tonight?"

"And have me risk being stuck with you if the track gets washed out before morning? No way!"

"Please?" She hated begging, but hated even more the prospect of waking Emma and Jamie and then trying to maneuver the Cutlass downhill in the stormy dark. And where to go from there? She suppressed a shudder. "I promise," she said, "I'll be out of here first thing in the morning."

His lips compressed so tightly they almost disappeared.

"All right," he snapped. "You can use the sitting room and the main floor powder room, just for tonight. But in the morning, you're history. Understood?"

"Heard and understood." She almost added a sarcastic 'sir,' but thought better of it. He was, after all, doing her a favor. So she just said, "Thank you. And thank you for agreeing to pay Chance's debts—I'll pay you back no matter how long it takes...."

But he'd already taken off, heading for the kitchen. His steps were purposeful. The steps of a man who knew where he was going and would let no one stand in his way.

Sarah slumped, feeling as if she'd been put through a wringer. But she'd achieved one goal—though it wasn't the main one that had drawn her here, the one that was far more important than borrowing money to pay off Chance's debts.

He'd never know her real reason for seeking him out. He'd never know how she'd hoped and prayed that Jedidiah Morgan would turn out to be a kindly man. A man who'd give his brother's family a warm welcome and let her stay at his home, with her children, till such time as she could once more cope with the difficult time that lay ahead.

What a fool she'd been. 'Kindly' was the very last word anyone would use to describe Jedidiah Morgan. The man was heartless. And whatever the cause of the estrangement between him and his brother, it was obvious the bitterness of it still remained, even now that Chance was gone.

Jed stared out into the dark, his hands braced against the side frames of his bedroom window.

Chance was dead.

It was the last thing he'd expected to hear.

Six years now since Jeralyn's death. Six years since his younger brother had fled and disappeared without a trace. Six years during which time he'd let his hatred of Chance build and build and build till now it almost consumed him.

His lips twisted in a bitter smile. So…Chance had never changed. Even in death, he left trouble in his wake. ''A mountain of unpaid bills,'' she'd called it. Well, to Sarah Morgan it might seem like a mountain; to him it was peanuts. And he was glad to pay the bill. Anything to get rid of that woman and her family, get them off the mountain.

All he wanted, in this life, was to be left alone.

CHAPTER TWO

SARAH woke next morning to the sound of a terse voice saying, "I'm going down the mountain to check that the road hasn't been washed out. I'll be back in twenty minutes."

Before she'd even blinked the sleep from her eyes, the sitting-room door snapped shut. And seconds later, she heard the front door slam.

Pushing aside her blanket, she sat up on the low-slung sofa. She hadn't drawn the curtains last night, and the room was now filled with gray shadows.

The children were still asleep, Emma on a love seat, Jamie in the depths of a recliner. Sarah felt her heart ache as she looked at them.

They'd adored Chance, and his death had left a big hole in their lives, a hole she tried her best to fill by lavishing all her love on them. But was it enough? She'd been eight when her own father had died, and the loss had been devastating. Years had passed before she'd finally given up hoping that by some miracle he would come back.

Now she was a single mom with a dream that seemed as out of reach as the stars: to have her children grow up in a warm and happy two-parent family.

Rising with a sigh, she tucked her hair behind her ears and crossed to the window. Rain bucketed down and the gale screamed around the corners. She shivered. Not a day to be traveling—

A movement just beyond her Cutlass caught her attention. Jedidiah Morgan was striding across the forecourt, his hair flattened by rain, his rangy frame encased in a navy anorak and jeans. At his heels loped Max. They were headed toward a Range Rover parked under a tree.

As she watched, he opened the driver's door. The dog leaped up into the vehicle; Jedidiah jumped up after him.

White gravel chips spurted from the wheels as he took off—in a hurry, Sarah thought gloomily, to be rid of her.

Emma stirred.

Sarah went over to sit on the edge of the love seat. "Good morning, honey." She cuddled her daughter, savoring the sleepy scent from her warm skin. "Time to get up."

As Emma feathered her tousled hair from her face with spread fingers, her pink cloth doll slid to the floor. Sarah bent to pick it up. Chance had bought the doll for Emma the day she was born, but it had remained nameless till Emma was over a year old, when she'd held it out one day and said proudly, "Girl!" The name had stuck.

Sarah set Girl on the coffee table, and as she did, Jamie stirred. Drowsily, he opened his eyes.

"Good morning, sweetie!" Sarah scooped him up and gave him a big hug.

He twined his arms around her neck. "I's hungry."

"Me, too," Emma said. "Starving!"

Sarah slid Jamie to the floor, and Emma grabbed his hand. "C'mon, Jamie," she said. "I know where to go!"

The kitchen smelled of coffee, but the coffeepot had been washed and the table was bare. If Sarah had hoped her host might have set out a breakfast for them, her hopes were dashed. The man was making it clear, in every possible way, that they were not welcome in his home.

She made scrambled eggs and toast for Emma and Jamie, and after pouring herself a glass of milk, she downed her daily quota of vitamin pills. Then tuning out the children's chatter, she moved to stand at the window.

Through the rain, she could see the mountain slope, dark with evergreens. On a sunny day, she reflected, the view would be awesome.

But she wouldn't be here to see it on any sunny day. She was to be out of this house within the hour.

Normally a cheerful, optimistic person, she felt dread settle over her. It was a scary world for a single mom with hardly any money; and especially for one in her situation, with no place to call home....

Though that wasn't strictly true. There was always Wynthrop. But the thought of returning to that house—where she would be even less welcome than she was here—made her very soul shudder.

"Mom," Emma said, "did our uncle come home yet?"

Sarah reined in her depressing thoughts. "Yes, he came home last night."

"Are we going to stay here awhile?"

"No, honey. We'll be leaving as soon as he returns. He's taken a drive down the mountain track to make sure the rain didn't wash it out."

"So he'll be back shortly?"

"Yes, he'll be back shortly."

When he hadn't come back in an hour, Sarah felt uneasy.

After a couple of hours, she was nibbling her thumbnail, a habit she'd broken when she was thirteen. The man should have been home by now. On her own drive up the mountain—on an unfamiliar road in the stormy dark—she'd taken, at most, fifteen minutes. Where could he be?

She paced the sitting room, sidestepping Jamie who was lying on the carpet, playing with his trucks. Emma stood at the window, hands pressed to the sill, shifting impatiently from one foot to the other. The child had spent the past couple of hours reading, but now she was restless.

Just as her mother was restless.

"Mom, there's a police car coming up the drive."

"A *police* car?"

"Yup."

Sarah hurried over to the window in time to see the car pull up beside her own. A uniformed officer stepped out.

Emma pressed her nose to the windowpane. "What do you think he wants, Mom?"

"Wait here. I'll find out."

"I want to come!"

"I want you to stay here." If something was wrong, she didn't want Emma to hear it. "Keep an eye on Jamie."

Emma pouted. But she did as she was told.

The doorbell rang.

The last time Sarah had answered the door to a

police officer had been on the day of Chance's death. A sick feeling swam in her stomach as she crossed the foyer; a feeling that intensified when she opened the door and saw the serious expression on the young officer's face.

"Ma'am, I'm Constable Trammer. You're…?"

"Mrs. Morgan. Sarah Morgan."

"You're the wife of Jedidiah Morgan?"

"No, his sister-in-law."

"I'm afraid there's been an accident, Mrs. Morgan. Down at the foot of the mountain, at the four-way intersection. A truck went through a stop sign and knocked Mr. Morgan's Range Rover off the road. The trucker's unhurt, but Mr. Morgan…"

Déjà vu. The same disembodied feeling that had assailed her when she'd been told about Chance's death threatened to undo Sarah now. She grabbed the edge of the door for support.

"He's been injured, ma'am, and has been taken by ambulance to St. Mary's Hospital in Kentonville."

Injured. Not dead.

Sarah closed her eyes, letting relief wash over her. When she opened them again, the constable was frowning.

"You okay?" he asked.

Abstractedly, she gestured his question aside. "Are Mr. Morgan's injuries life threatening?"

"He got a bang on the side of his head and with that kind of injury there's always a risk. He was unconscious when we got to him."

"The hospital…where did you say it was?"

"Kentonville. Ten miles west of here, on the river. Hospital's right at this end of town. You can't miss it."

St. Mary's Hospital was a peach-colored stucco building, situated between the Kenton Motel and the municipal library.

Sarah learned at the information desk that her brother-in-law was in room 345. She ushered the children to the elevator, and when they emerged on the third floor, she spotted room 345 across the way. But as she led the children toward it, she was accosted by a stout, redheaded nurse who came out from behind her desk.

"May I ask," she said, "where you're going?"

Sarah paused. "I'm Sarah Morgan. I've come to visit my—"

"Visiting hours don't start till two. Who was it you wanted to see?"

"Jedidiah Morgan. Room 345. Sorry we're not supposed to be here—we'll come back later."

"Mr. Morgan's doctor wants him to rest today—it would really be best if he has no visitors. He's had *quite* a knock."

A reprieve. Sarah felt a surge of guilty relief. "In that case," she said, "I guess we'll be getting home."

"If at all possible," the nurse offered, "Mr. Morgan will be discharged tomorrow—we're *seriously* short of beds. Phone in the morning, and if he's been given the all clear, you can pick him up. He won't be fit to drive…and anyway, from what I've heard, his vehicle's a write-off."

Goose bumps rose on Sarah's skin as memories of another accident swept into her mind: Chance's car, too, had been a write-off. Unfortunately, no angels had been looking out for him as they had been today for his brother.

"Are you okay?" the nurse asked. "You look pale."

Sarah's smile was wan. "It's been a shock."

The nurse hesitated and then said in a whisper, "Tell you what. The patient's asleep right now, but I'll look after the kids if you just want to have a peek at him."

An offer, Sarah realized wryly, she could hardly refuse under the circumstances. Faking a grateful smile, she said, "Thanks," and crossed to the open doorway of room 345.

Her brother-in-law lay flat on his back on a narrow bed, his eyes closed, his arms out over the covers, his hands clasped over his chest. If he had a bump on his head, Sarah reflected, it was concealed by his thick black hair. His face was chalk-white, his pallor accentuated by his dark, unshaven jaw.

Hardly aware of what she was doing, she moved quietly over to the bed and stood there, studying him.

His lips, she noticed, were dry.

Sensual lips, and thinner than Chance's. The sooty black eyelashes were thicker than Chance's; the ridge on the nose more pronounced; the jaw firmer.

So the two brothers weren't as alike as she'd initially thought—

"Who the hell," asked a slurred voice, "are you?"

The patient was *not* asleep. Startled, Sarah braced herself for the verbal attack that would surely ensue when he recognized her. When she saw his blank expression, her tension eased slightly. He must be hovering in some twilight zone, she figured; either groggy from the accident or drowsy from medication.

"Hush." Impulsively, she set her hand on his. "I'm sorry, I've disturbed you. And I shouldn't even be here."

He twisted his hand and trapped her wrist with strong fingers.

"Who *are* you?" His question came out raspingly. "And what's going on?"

How much should she tell him? Better to say nothing. The truth might set his blood pressure skyrocketing.

"You'll find out everything," she said quickly, "once you're feeling better." Tugging her hand free, she backed away. "I'm not even supposed to be here!"

"Wait!"

Ignoring his urgent command, she whirled and fled out to the corridor.

The nurse was at the elevator with the children, and when she saw Sarah, she pressed the elevator button. The doors glided open just as Sarah got there.

With a murmured "Thanks," Sarah guided the children inside and pressed the lobby button.

"Bye, kids!" The nurse gave the children a wave and then said to Sarah, just as the doors began to swish shut, "I'll tell your husband when he wakes up that you paid him a visit."

Sarah blinked and then said quickly, "Oh, but he's—"

The doors clicked into place.

"—not my husband."

Too late. The elevator had already begun its descent.

He drifted in and out of consciousness, with time meaning nothing to him. He gathered he was in the hospital, that he'd been involved in a car accident—not his fault, that of the other driver. He also gathered that apart from a few bruises, his only injury was a blow to his head, which he'd sustained on impact with the other vehicle.

Nurses checked on him periodically, but despite his attempts to engage them in conversation, they had little time to chat. He also had the vaguest recollection of seeing a blond angel hovering over him at one point.

He knew that in near-death experiences, people sometimes saw a tunnel of white light with figures beckoning them. He'd apparently not been near death and he'd seen no white light, but the angel had spoken to him in a husky, melodic voice. He recalled her saying apologetically that she wasn't supposed to be there.

Perhaps she'd come to his room by mistake, thinking he was soon to be not of this world. And then discovered she'd been wrong. Even angels must make mistakes.

He dreamed of her that night; and when he wakened in the morning, the dream remained vividly in his mind.

A mind that was now, thankfully, lucid....

Except for one thing.

One problem.

And it was a whopper!

He had no idea who he was.

He knew he'd been in an accident because someone had told him; but he had no memory of it.

And he had no memory of anything that had happened prior to the crash.

Hell's teeth. He lay back on his pillow, stunned. What a dilemma. Who *was* he?

He was still pondering the question when a tall gray-haired doctor appeared at his bedside. Behind him hovered a nurse.

"Rasmussen," the man said bluntly. And proceeded to give him a thorough examination. "Right, Mr. Morgan—"

Ah, now he knew his name. Or at least his surname. It was a start.

"—you can go home this morning. Where do you live?"

Before he could answer, the nurse piped up, "The patient has a place on Whispering Mountain—about ten miles from here."

Well, he reflected, at least he wasn't homeless!

"He shouldn't do much for himself for the next couple of days. He'll be a bit off balance. Does he have someone to look after him?"

Did he? The patient turned a keen gaze on the nurse, interested to hear the answer.

"Oh, yes, Doctor. Mr. Morgan has a wife—"

He had a wife? Odd, he didn't *feel* married.

"—isn't that right, Jedidiah?" The nurse threw him a saccharine-sweet smile.

Jedidiah. What kind of a mother would stick her son with a name like that? "Oh, sure," he said brightly. "A wife."

"Good," the doctor said. "Now take it easy for the next few days. You've had a nasty knock. No drinking, no driving. And stay quiet. Take a break from work."

"Sure." Work? Did he work? Or was he perhaps a dilettante playboy? Surreptitiously, hopefully, he turned over his hands and stole a glance at his palms—

Hey, would you look at those *calluses*! Those were not the hands of a man who lived a life of glitz and glamour.

But they were the hands of a man who didn't ask for directions when he was lost. That much he knew, and the knowledge was innate. It probably went all the way back to caveman days, when no caveman worth his salt would have asked another caveman where the best buffalo were roaming.

"Any questions?" The doctor stood poised to leave.

"Nope."

"Remember anything of the accident?"

Jedidiah shook his head. And winced as pain sliced through it.

"It might come back, but probably won't. Most people find that because of the trauma it's blocked out of their minds permanently. You may also find that the swelling around your brain will have caused further memory loss. As the swelling subsides, those memories—your personal memories—should eventually return." The doctor was halfway to the door. "Any problems, just give me a call."

"Will do. And thanks."

After the doctor left, the nurse said, "You'll find

all your clothes in that locker by your bed.'' She headed for the door.

Jedidiah said, ''Hold on a minute.''

She turned.

''Has my…wife called this morning?''

''She called first thing and then she called again, just after ten. I told her I'd phone back after the doctor had seen you. I'll call her now and tell her she can come pick you up.''

''Call me a cab instead.''

''But your wife—''

''I want to surprise her.''

The nurse beamed. ''I'll call you that cab. And I'll come back shortly to wheel you downstairs.''

As the sound of the nurse's brisk footsteps faded along the corridor, Jedidiah swung his legs off the bed, then paused as a wave of giddiness assailed him. When he finally stood, the floor seemed to tilt. He grasped the bed rail, and once he felt steadier, he moved to his locker.

When he looked at his clothes, they were unfamiliar to him. Blue jeans, denim shirt, navy jacket. It was as if he'd never seen them before.

Yet he knew what they were called; and when he withdrew his black leather wallet from his hip pocket, he knew it was called a wallet. Odd how his mind had retained that kind of information, yet all his personal memories seemed lost.

He unfolded the wallet and riffled curiously through its contents. He found over seventy dollars in bills; a few credit cards; a receipt for gas. And his driver's license. He noted his address—Morgan's Hope, Whispering Mountain, B.C. He checked his

birth date against the date on the gas receipt and figured he was almost thirty-five. Looking at his photo
was like looking at the face of a stranger—a stranger
with dark hair and an even darker scowl.

He searched further, hoping to find a picture of his
wife, but no luck. He slid the wallet back into the
pocket, his mind swirling with questions.

When he got home, he'd get his wife to answer
them.

He scraped a rueful hand through his hair. His wife.

He couldn't *wait* to see what she looked like!

''Mom, how come you're unloading all that stuff
from the car and bringing it into our uncle's house?''

Over the bulky bag in her arms, Sarah peeked at
Emma and Jamie, who were zooming Jamie's Tonka
trucks over the foyer carpet. ''When I called the nurse
she said that when your uncle gets home, he'd need
taking care of for a few days. I plan to look after
him.''

Even if he didn't want her to, Sarah reflected as
nervousness churned her stomach. But she hoped he
wouldn't be up to arguing. In fact, she was counting
on it. She desperately needed time to regroup, time
to decide where to go when she left Morgan's Hope.

''When are we going to the hospital?'' Jamie
asked.

''The nurse promised to phone me after the doctor
had made his rounds. I'm surprised she hasn't called
yet.''

''It'll be a lovely surprise for our uncle,'' Emma
said happily, ''to find that we've moved ourselves in!''

*   *   *

"Need a hand, buddy?" The cabdriver squinted against the sun as he peered up through his open window at Jedidiah, who was tucking his wallet away. "You seemed a bit unsteady on your pins, back there at the hospital."

"Thanks, I'm okay."

"Nice place you got here."

"Mmm." Jedidiah's attention was fixed on the rusty blue Cutlass parked by the front door. His wife's? How come she drove a dilapidated old vehicle when apparently his own vehicle had been a late-model Range Rover?

The cabbie gestured toward Max, who had also been a passenger in his cab but was now standing by his master. "Amazing that your dog was hanging around waiting for you in the hospital grounds. He must've followed the ambulance all the way to town yesterday. Lucky you had a name tag on him, prove he was yours. Sure are faithful, those mutts."

"Yeah." Jedidiah set a hand on Max's head and the animal looked up at him adoringly.

"Better'n a woman any day!" With a quick grin, the cabbie put his vehicle in gear and drove away.

Jedidiah's eyes were thoughtful as he walked with an unsteady gait to the house. Inside waited his wife. Her name was Sarah, according to a remark dropped by the redheaded nurse when she'd wheeled him down to the entrance. And Sarah had visited him yesterday, the nurse had confided, though he'd been too out of it to know it.

If he had seen her, would he have recognized her? He doubted he would....

He remembered nothing of her. Nothing of his past.

Remembered nothing of this house.

"Nice place," the cabbie had remarked, and he'd been right. It was a very nice place indeed, with clean lines and an attractive symmetry to it. He liked the pink brick walls, the white trim, the indigo-blue door. And he liked the arrangement of potted shrubs set around the entrance.

Everywhere he looked, he saw order.

And money.

He glanced at his palms again, and frowned. Those calluses. What the heck kind of work did he do that he could afford such a place?

Squaring his shoulders, he said, "C'mon, Max. Let's go inside and find out."

But Max had loped away into the forest.

The front door was unlocked.

Jedidiah opened it. Closed it. Took off his shoes. Stepped forward into the foyer.

And that's when he saw them.

Two children, a boy of around three and a girl maybe a couple of years older, sitting on the carpet over by the staircase, playing with blocks. They were so intent on what they were doing they didn't notice him.

He stood, watching. Fascinated.

The boy was slightly built, with a sweep of ash-blond hair. He was wearing jeans and a red sweater. The girl was sturdier, but her hair was equally blond and styled in a long braid. She, too, was wearing jeans, but her sweater was blue with a pattern of snowflakes.

He cleared his throat.

The little girl looked up.

She stared at him for a long moment, her beautiful gray eyes startled, and then she cried, "*Daddy*!"

The boy turned sharply. His eyes were as gray as the girl's, and at sight of him, they lit up.

"Da-da!" He scrambled to his feet, and for a moment the two children stood rooted to the spot. Then the girl threw out her arms and with a shriek of joy ran toward him. The boy followed suit.

What could he do but swing them up and hug them? How were they to know he didn't recognize them? How were they to know he felt as if they were strangers to him?

He swung them around and then swung them down again.

The little girl ran to the stairs and yelled, "Mom! Mom! Daddy's come back!"

Jedidiah followed, his heart beating in slow, heavy thuds as he waited for this woman who was his wife.

Her voice preceded her. "Honey, what are you…?"

And then she appeared, hurrying out onto the landing.

She glanced down, frowning.

And stopped dead at the sight of him.

She looked stunned; more stunned even than her daughter had been.

And every vestige of color seeped from her face.

"Oh, hi." Her voice was flat. "It's you."

CHAPTER THREE

Wow, that was some warm welcome!

Jedidiah grasped the knob of the newel post for support as shock hurtled his giddiness to new heights. And added to his shock was jaw-dropping awe: this woman was gorgeous.

Not only was she gorgeous, she was the vision who'd appeared at his hospital bedside. No angel, but his wife.

He gaped at her as she started slowly down the stairs.

Sarah Morgan was a fragile blonde, with smooth, silky hair parted on the left. It curved out bell-like around her heart-shaped face, ending in a loose wave that brought the tips in to brush against her neck then flip out again. Her skin was clear, her nose was straight…and her gray eyes were fixed on him warily.

"I was going to drive to the hospital and pick you up." Her voice was low and melodic, with a husky timbre.

He found it incredibly sexy.

Something stirred deep inside him.

"The nurse said she'd call me." She trailed her left hand down the railing as she descended. A delicate gold band glinted on her ring finger. "After the doctor had checked you out."

She was straight shouldered and leggy, fine boned and elegant. And though the voluminous shirt billow-

34

ing out over her jeans concealed her shape, he had no problem envisioning a curvy little figure under the crisp white cotton.

She'd reached the last step and was only an arm's span away. To his astonishment, he saw she was trembling.

He reached out and took possession of her left hand. She started. Tried to tug it free. As she did, her perfume drifted to him, sweet roses spiced with carnation. Feminine and tantalizing. He tightened his grip.

"Well, hi, Mrs. Morgan," he said softly, caressing her wedding band with the pad of his thumb. "How about a 'Welcome home' kiss for the injured warrior?"

Her lips parted in a gasp.

Her eyes sparked with indignation.

Her body language screamed rejection.

He did a mental double take. Had they quarreled before the accident? If so, whose fault had it been?

His, apparently!

Oh, what the heck—whoever had been at fault, it was time to make up. And the making up, he figured with a sense of pleasurable anticipation, would be fun.

Keeping her wrist trapped with one hand, he slid the fingers of the other through her hair to cup her head. And before she could catch her breath, he leaned forward and claimed her parted pink lips with his own.

From a foggy distance, he heard a child's giggle.

"Jamie," his daughter whispered, "Daddy's kissing Mommie."

But Mommie, Jedidiah realized with an uneasy jolt,

wasn't kissing Daddy back. And he'd enjoyed only a brief taste of satin-soft, heavenly sweet lips when she wrenched herself away from him.

Her next move stunned him: she wiped her mouth with the back of her hand. And what stunned him even more than her undisguised disgust was the rage in her glare.

"That was inexcusable!" she hissed. "I know you want to get rid of me, but that's a despicable way to go about it—taking advantage of me. *Especially* in front of the children!"

"Get rid of you?" He blinked. "Why should I want to get rid of you?"

Her eyes went blank for five seconds. Then they took on a scornful expression. "So you've changed your tune now that you need help. Oh, you didn't have to bother with all that playacting. I'm not about to leave you in the lurch."

"Sarah, I have to tell you—"

"Go to bed," she snapped. "You look as if you're going to pass out at any minute." Pausing only to scoop up the little boy—his son!—she said, "Emma, come with me to the kitchen. I'll make us all some lunch."

The little girl—his daughter!—trotted after Sarah.

Head spinning, he watched them go. He didn't *want* any lunch. All he wanted was to lie down. But first, he had to tell his wife he'd lost his memory. Then he'd have her fill him in on everything he'd forgotten. And the first thing he wanted to know was: why was she so angry with him?

Legs wobbly as rubber, he made his way across the foyer, following the fast-fading sound of voices.

''Mom—'' that was Emma ''—I wanted to go up-stairs with Daddy!''

He turned into a corridor and saw a room ahead with the door swinging half-shut. The voices now came from beyond it.

''We have to talk, Emma.'' Sarah's voice came faintly. ''That man—he's not your daddy.''

Jedidiah stumbled. Almost fell. He righted himself, swore under his breath—what breath he had left! He wasn't the child's father? Then whose child was she?

''He is *too* my daddy!''

''No, your daddy's gone to Heaven. You *know* that.''

''But he's come back!'' Emma started to cry. ''Daddy's come back!''

''Honey, he's not your daddy. And he's not Jamie's daddy, either—''

Now the boy started to cry, a keening wail that drowned out the heartrending sobs jerking from his sister.

Jedidiah felt as if the carpet had been swept out from under his feet. Was this real? Or was he still in his hospital bed under the influence of some mind-bending drug?

''Listen to me.'' Sarah's voice was urgent, with an edge of panic. ''Both of you. I'm going to explain.''

He cocked his head and his ears. This he wanted to hear. But a shadow fell over the open doorway, and a second later the kitchen door shut with a sharp click.

He eased his way along the corridor and stopped at the door. Pressing his ear to it, he listened.

All he could hear was a murmur.

Not one word was intelligible.

Oh, this was great. His wife wasn't speaking to him, and his children were some other man's.

But now was not the time to ask for explanations; not with Jamie and Emma around. They were already upset enough. He'd wait till he got Sarah on her own.

Turning, he felt a great emptiness in his heart as he made his way to the stairs. He'd thought, when he'd come back to this house, that it was a home. A home, with a wife who loved him. What he had walked into was a situation as bleak as it was depressing: a house with a woman who despised him, and two children who belonged to some other man.

By the time he'd climbed the stairs, he could hardly see straight. He staggered into the first bedroom he came to, and after clumsily stripping to his briefs, he aimed himself toward the bed. It was queen-size, with a puffy hunter-green duvet.

He tugged the duvet aside, fell onto the mattress.

And passed into oblivion.

Sarah sat on the ladder-back chair, with Jamie on her knee and Emma standing in front of her. Emma clutched Girl to her chest as she listened to her mother's explanation.

"So you see," Sarah finished, "Mr. Morgan isn't Daddy, but his older brother. And that's why he looks like Daddy."

"I thought Daddy had come down from Heaven," Emma said sadly.

"Da-da," pronounced Jamie firmly, "is back."

Sarah sighed. She believed that Emma now understood the situation; Jamie, obviously, did not.

"He's your uncle, Jamie. And I don't want to hear one more word about it." She got up and set him on his booster seat. "After we have lunch, Emma, I'm going to put Jamie down for a nap. You, too—"

"I don't want a nap!" Emma protested.

"Yesterday was a long day," Sarah said. "And you were up till after midnight. No arguments."

She needed to talk to Jedidiah Morgan. Needed to set him straight about a few things. And she didn't want the children around when she did.

The man had a nerve, she reflected tautly as she opened a can of tomato soup; to kiss her like that, thinking it would sweeten her up.

She paused, the can momentarily forgotten as her mind flicked back. It had been so unexpected—the last thing in the world she'd thought he had in mind when she joined him at the foot of the stairs. Certainly she hadn't been thinking about kissing. She'd been thinking how shattered he looked; how exhausted.

Huh!

Lips compressed, she poured the soup into a pan. Not so exhausted that he couldn't stir up the energy to grab her and give her a bone-melting kiss—

Bone-melting?

A hot blush rose to her cheeks. She'd purposely avoided thinking about that kiss and the effect it had had on her. His lips had been sensual and smooth, his scent musky and male. For a mind-stopping moment she'd been tempted to succumb to his advances. Lord only knew how she'd managed to resist.

But thank heaven she had.

Jedidiah Morgan was, she realized, just like his brother—he could turn on the con man's charm when it suited him. But she wasn't about to fall for the Morgan charm again. Not now. Not ever.

She put the pan on the burner and switched the burner on. She'd take him some lunch as soon as she'd fed the children. And once he'd eaten, she'd let him know that if he wanted her to stay and look after him for a few days, first they had to establish some ground rules.

"Mom." Emma paused with her soup spoon halfway to her mouth. "I think I hear a dog outside."

"A doggie?" Jamie's eyes gleamed.

As Jamie spoke, Sarah heard a sharp yelp, followed by a scrabbling sound against the back door.

She sighed. "That'll be Max—your uncle's dog." She'd forgotten all about the black Lab—but she certainly hadn't forgotten its aggressive reaction to her when they'd met.

"I didn't know Uncle Jed had a dog. Can I let him in?" Emma asked eagerly.

"Hang on," Sarah said. "He didn't take to me when I met him so I must see if I can make friends with him first."

She opened cupboards, looking for dog food, and under the sink found a red bowl and a bag of dry dog food. After tipping a generous measure into the bowl, she carried the dish to the door.

Then taking a deep breath, she opened the door.

Max started to growl when he saw her, but she said, "Good dog!" in a confident, reassuring tone and held out the bowl.

He immediately ignored her and dove right at the food, almost knocking the bowl from her hand. She stepped back and he followed, his tail wagging like mad, his nose foraging in the bowl.

There, she thought with a chuckle, that wasn't so hard. Setting the dish on the floor, she leaned back against the counter and glanced at the children.

"What do you think?" she asked. "Isn't he beautiful?"

"Ooh, he's cool!" Emma said.

Jamie, who was crazy about dogs, stared at Max in wide-eyed wonder. "Can we *pet* him?" he asked breathlessly.

"Not while he's eating," Sarah said. "Let's leave him just now, and after your nap we'll see if he wants to play."

While searching for blankets the night before, Sarah had found there were five bedrooms upstairs. One was the master bedroom. The room next to it was apparently a guest room. The two across the way were unfurnished. And the fifth, at the end of the corridor, was a large room, decorated in yellow and furnished with twin beds.

It was to this room that she led Jamie and Emma when they went up for their nap. After tucking them in, she drew the curtains and made her way back along the corridor.

She paused at the master bedroom and tapped on the door. There was no response. Opening the door, she peeked in, intending to ask Jedidiah if he was ready for lunch.

He lay sprawled on the bed, out like a light.

And he'd probably remain that way for several hours, she reflected as she closed the door. And despite her distaste for his despicable attitude toward her, she felt a wave of compassion for him. He had, after all, undergone quite an ordeal. Sleep would do him good.

Jedidiah woke slowly.

To darkness.

And the sound of someone breathing.

Someone very close to him.

So close he could feel a warm breath fanning his cheek.

"Da-da?"

He turned his head. As his eyes adjusted, he saw Jamie standing by the bed, his small hands clutching the duvet.

"Hey, kid," Jedidiah whispered. "How's it going?"

"I's lost."

"Lost, huh?"

"Up!" The child stretched out his arms.

Jedidiah pulled him on board, and a second later the pajamaed figure was cuddled up beside him under the duvet. And in less than a minute, Jamie had drifted off to sleep.

Jedidiah peered at his watch. Almost nine.

Night or morning?

There was only one way to find out.

Easing himself carefully across the bed, he sat up, swung his legs over the edge of the mattress…

And winced.

A wild party had started up inside his head. The stereo beat throbbed against his temple with the insistency of a tom-tom calling a savage tribe to war.

He sat absolutely still till the pain subsided. Then slowly he got up and made his way to the window.

He edged back the curtain and saw that it was dark out.

Night, then.

Hauling on his jeans, he headed for the en suite bathroom—and it was only as he pushed open the door that he found himself wondering how he'd known it was there.

"Mom?"

Sarah looked up from the kitchen table, where she'd just emptied out her bag in a search for her antacid tablets. "Emma, what on earth do you want?"

"Isn't it morning?"

"No, it's not morning!"

"I woke up." The child yawned. "And Jamie was gone so I thought it was morning and I came down for breakfast."

Sarah frowned. "He's not in his bed?"

"And he's not in the bathroom." Emma yawned again. "Where's Max?"

"He's dozing in the sitting room." Sarah skimmed a glance at the monitor, which was lying on the countertop. She'd set it there after putting the children to bed...but darn it, with everything that had been happening, she'd forgotten to flick it on. She did it now.

"Let's go upstairs," she said. "I need to find him before he gets into mischief. I wonder if he went looking for that dog!"

When they reached the landing, Sarah noticed that the door to the master bedroom stood ajar. The room was in darkness, but she could see a pencil of light under the en suite door.

So…Jedidiah was up.

"C'mon, Mom, I want to go back to bed."

She ushered Emma back to her room, tucked her in, then began a swift search for Jamie. He wasn't in any of the bedrooms. Could he have wandered downstairs?

She hurried back along the corridor and almost bumped into Jedidiah as he emerged from his room.

He was wearing only jeans, and even in her state of anxiety over Jamie, she couldn't help noticing what a fantastic body the man had—lean, tanned, muscled, with crisp black hair covering his chest and tapering down…

She sucked in a lungful of air and shot her gaze back to his face. "Excuse me." Her voice had a Marilyn Monroe breathiness that appalled her. "I wasn't looking where I was going. I've lost Jamie and—"

"He's in here—he's asleep."

"Oh. I'm sorry if he woke you—"

"No problem."

She made to walk around him. "I'll just get him—"

"Why don't you leave him?" He braced a hand against the door frame, halting her. "He's okay where he is."

There was something profoundly intimate about his stance. He wasn't touching her, but she felt trapped within his space, and he was so close she could smell the salty sweat from his skin. Feel the heat of it.

She cleared her throat and took a step sideways.

"He needs to be in the other room. I have the monitor set up so I can hear him."

"You obviously didn't hear him this time around!" He dropped his arm and, leaning languidly against the door frame, surveyed her with a gleam of amusement in his eyes.

"I'd forgotten to switch it on."

She walked around him and crossed to the bed. Scooping Jamie up carefully, she carried him to the door.

"I thought he might have gone looking for Max," she said. "I don't know where the dog's been, but he's back."

"He apparently followed the ambulance to the hospital and then hung around waiting for me. Was he hungry?"

"I've fed him."

"Good. Sarah…we need to talk. After you put Jamie down."

"I agree." Her eyes had taken on a haughty glitter. "There are certainly things we should discuss!"

Jed watched her stalk off along the corridor. She was a sparky little thing, this wife of his. It was going to be interesting, getting to know her. Kind of like courting her all over again. He found the prospect exhilarating.

After putting on a shirt, he made his way along to the landing. As he descended the stairs, he glanced around and found himself perplexed by what he saw.

Nothing about the interior of this house drew him. The place not only had a sterile quality, it gave a whole new dimension to the word "tidy." Something deep inside him ached to see a scarf tossed over the oak hall stand; fingerprints on the pristine white walls; even a fractional misalignment of the oil painting hanging sedately above the telephone table.

What kind of woman had he married that she needed such order in her life? Because he was pretty damned sure he wasn't the one who wanted it to be this way. He knew—he just knew!—that he couldn't have been comfortable in such barren surroundings.

Sarah Morgan was an enigma.

Shaking his head, he strolled along to the kitchen, but when he opened the door he did a double take. The room looked as if a bomb had hit it.

There was scarcely a square inch of surface area visible. Dirty dishes cluttered the sink. Toys were scattered on the floor. Children's clothes—underwear, shirts, socks—littered the countertops. And a spill of items from an open handbag took up most of the table.

The woman was not only an enigma, he decided with a feeling of shock, she had a split personality.

''Good grief!'' he muttered. And he was so busy taking it all in, he didn't hear footsteps coming up behind him.

''What's the matter?'' Sarah asked.

He turned to her. ''This place is a disaster area!''

Her face became scarlet. ''I'm sorry. Give me a minute and I'll have it tidied....''

Seeing her embarrassment, he felt like an ogre. A bewildered ogre. This was her kitchen: why was she being so apologetic? Was he, after all, a man who demanded that his wife keep their home neat as a pin despite the presence of two small children? Was *he* responsible for the unlived-in atmosphere that permeated their house? He hadn't thought so. Yet—

"Sit down," she said. "I'll clear up and then give you dinner."

"How about feeding me first, cleaning up after? I can't remember when I last ate!"

Which was not *all* he couldn't remember! But he'd get around to telling her that shortly.

"The children and I had meat loaf. So...meat loaf, potatoes, peas? I'll heat it in the microwave."

"Sounds great."

As she arranged some food on a plate and slid the plate into the microwave, he glanced at the items scattered on the table. Pens, pencils, a notebook. A packet of tissues. Three yellow suckers, two chocolate bars. Lipstick in a silver case. A child's pink hairbrush. A red bankbook, a blue vinyl wallet. A few loose coins, a five-dollar bill.

Idly, he flicked up the bill, intending to tuck it inside the wallet. But when the wallet fell open to reveal a photo behind a clear plastic window, he paused, his eyes fixed on the two people in the snap.

Sarah...and himself.

She was wearing an amethyst sundress, her blond hair cut gamine style. He was in cutoffs and a Rolling Stones T-shirt, his hair pulled back in a ponytail.

A *ponytail*? That didn't feel like his style—

"What do you think you're doing?" Sarah's voice was sharp.

"When was this taken?" He spread out the open wallet flat on the table and pushed it toward her.

"Six years ago. On our honeymoon."

"Where?"

"In San Francisco."

Her voice was tight and angry, but it held no hint of puzzlement…and that astonished him. Why wasn't she saying, "You know where that was taken! You were there!"?

But before he could speak, the microwave beeped. She swiveled her back to him, took out his dinner and set it on the table in front of him. Taking a knife and fork from a drawer in the island, she dumped them by his plate.

"Do you want a glass of milk?" she asked, curt as a waitress who expected no tip.

"Thanks."

Equally curtly, she served the milk.

Then keeping her eyes averted, she transferred all her belongings from the table to her bag and, after setting the bag on a chair, stashed the dirty dishes in the dishwasher.

Silently, he ate, all the while wondering at her odd reaction to his questions but coming up with no explanation.

By the time he'd cleaned his plate and polished off his milk, she'd tidied the kitchen and was tossing the last Lego block into its container.

"Dessert?" she asked as she swept up his plate and glass. "We had apple crisp."

"No thanks. I don't eat dessert."

How did he know that?

And more importantly, how come she didn't?

Oh, he was getting weary of this whole thing. Tilting back his chair, he watched her through speculative eyes as she crossed to the window. Outside, the night was dark and all he could see was black beyond the shiny pane.

"Sit down," he said. "Let's talk."

"Half a sec." Turning sideways, she reached up for the cord to close the venetian blind. And as she did, her billowing shirt floated up.

Revealing her figure.

In profile.

Jedidiah stared, hardly able to believe his eyes.

He'd thought, when she walked down the stairs to greet him on his return from the hospital, that under her oversize shirt, her figure would be delectably slim and curvy.

It certainly wasn't slim. But oh, yes, it was curvy.

Curvy didn't even *begin* to describe his wife's figure.

It was obvious to anyone with half a brain that Sarah Morgan was pregnant. And if he knew anything about babies, this one was due to arrive in the not-too-distant future.

Only one question remained to be answered...and now was the time to ask it!

He got up from his chair and cleared his throat loudly.

Aggressively.

She turned, then looked at him with her eyebrows raised.

"I see," he said, "that you're pregnant. If you don't mind my asking—" his voice rang with challenge "—who is the father of *this* lucky child?"

CHAPTER FOUR

SARAH'S mind tottered in disbelief.

Of all the men she'd ever met, Jedidiah Morgan was undoubtedly the most despicable—the most despicable and the most insulting!

"Who do you think?" She spiked him with an icy gaze.

His Adam's apple bobbed convulsively. "The same man who fathered Jamie and Emma?"

"Right!" She snatched up his plate, and china clattered ominously as she shoved it into the dishwasher. "Who else?"

Whirling around, she planted her hands on her hips, ready to do battle. But at the sight of his dazed expression, she felt the edges of her outrage wilt. The man had been through a lot; she should be taking that into consideration and making allowances.

Heaving out a frustrated sigh, she said, "You shouldn't be upsetting yourself. You're supposed to be convalescing. Why don't you get yourself back upstairs and go to—"

"Bed?" He cocked his head and fixed taunting green eyes on her. "Sure," he drawled. "If you'll come with me."

Sarah gasped. And felt her wilted outrage blossom to vigorous life again. "You have a nerve—"

"I do?" His air had become one of injured innocence. "If you don't want to sleep with me, why have you stayed?"

Jedidiah Morgan had an ego the size of Whispering Mountain. "I've stayed," she snapped, "because you need looking after."

He shoved his chair back and got unsteadily to his feet. "What I don't understand," he said, "is why I've let you stay on here in the first place when you're obviously a woman with no morals—"

"*What*?"

"This whole situation is beyond my comprehension. You welcomed me home this morning with less enthusiasm than a chicken would welcome a wolf to the henhouse. You won't kiss me, far less share my bed. You've got two kids—with another on the way—and you admit none of them is mine. What kind of wife does that make you? And what disturbs me even more—what kind of man am I that I haven't kicked you out before now?" He swayed and put a hand on the countertop to keep himself upright. "I'm your *husband*, woman! Doesn't that mean anything to you?"

"My *husband*?" Sarah stared at him. "Are you out of your *mind*?"

He stared back at her, the tension between them so tightly sprung it vibrated. They stood there, glaring at each other, with no sound in the kitchen but the hum of the refrigerator, the rain drumming against the windowpanes...

And their rapid breathing.

He spoke first.

"I'm not your husband?" The words came out in

a thin, strangled way as if someone was pressing on his windpipe.

"No." She barely recognized her own raspy voice. "Of *course* you're not!"

"Are you saying…we're not married?"

Sarah drew in a sharp breath. Was that what this had all been about? Jedidiah Morgan believed she was his wife? If so, the injury to his head must truly have scrambled his brain.

"Married?" Her laugh was dry. "In your dreams, Mr. Morgan."

"Have we…ever been married? To each other?"

"Not in this lifetime! Nor in any other—" she rolled her eyes heavenward "—God willing!"

"I think—" he slumped sideways against the counter "—that it's time for me to put my cards on the table."

His face had become putty-colored and he looked as if he was going to pass out. "*I* think," she said quickly, "it's time you went back to bed."

"Alone?" He cocked an eyebrow and she saw a wicked glitter in his beautiful green eyes.

"Alone," she said firmly.

"Damn!"

He hadn't realized how utterly done-in he was till he was once again in bed.

Flat on his back, hands clasped behind his head, he waited for this woman-who-wasn't-his-wife to return. After seeing him to his room, she'd said she was going to check on the children but would be right back.

His mind was a welter of confusion. How much

simpler it would've been if he'd come clean when he arrived home.

I've lost my memory, he should've called up to her when she'd appeared on the landing. *Fill me in, honey!*

Instead, he'd succumbed to this stubborn male ego thing, refusing to reveal any sign of weakness.

''Feeling better?'' Sarah's crisp voice came from the doorway.

''Marginally.'' He watched as she approached the bed.

She pulled a cushioned chair over beside him and sat down. Cupping her hands primly over her knees, she leaned forward and fixed him with a serious look. ''Jedidiah—''

''That's a helluva mouthful. Let's cut it back to Jed.''

''Okay. *Jed.* You said you were going to put your cards on the table. I think it's time for me to see them.''

''It's way past time.'' His smile was sheepish. ''What happened—well, that bump on my head must've jarred my brain because when I woke up in the hospital, I found I'd lost my memory.''

Her eyes widened. ''You mean…everything's a blank?''

''You got it.''

For a long moment she just stared at him. And then she said, ''That's terrible! But…what made you think we were married?''

''According to one of the nurses, my wife had visited.''

''That must have been the nurse who let me pop

in to see you. She *assumed* I was your wife, but I didn't get the chance to set her straight.''

''Red-haired, buxom?''

''That's the one.''

He nodded. ''Okay, but in addition to that, when I got here, the kids called me Daddy. How do you explain that?''

''Because at first glance you do look very like their father.''

''I do?''

She swallowed. ''He…Chance…was your brother.''

''I have a brother?''

''Had. Chance died seven months ago.''

Jed saw a shadow flit over her gray eyes and he felt a surge of sympathy. He guessed she was still grieving. What a shock it must have been to lose her husband especially while she was so young.

He wondered how he himself had reacted when he'd learned of Chance's death. He felt nothing now—just a vague sensation of guilt that he didn't even remember he'd had a brother.

''He was killed in a car accident,'' Sarah went on quietly. ''He was twenty-nine.''

''How long were you married?''

''Almost six years.''

''So…the honeymoon picture…that was you and Chance?''

She nodded.

He mulled this over. ''So…I guess you and I have known each other for some time?''

''We'd never met…till the other night.''

''How come?''

''You and Chance didn't keep in touch. I knew you were older than he was and I knew you had a place on Whispering Mountain—and I knew you lost your parents when he was twenty. But other than that, he would tell me nothing.''

''What made you decide to come to Morgan's Hope and—'' Jed broke off as a shaft of pain sliced through his head. He waited for the pain to ease, but when it did it left a dull, heavy throbbing in its wake. The effort to think became onerous. He rubbed a hand over his temple. So much to absorb. So much to try to understand.

''Are you okay?'' Sarah's concerned voice seemed to come from far away.

He closed his eyes. ''D'you mind if we finish this talk later?''

''Of course not.'' He heard the scrape of chair legs on the carpet. ''It's been too much to take in all at once.'' He felt a light, comforting touch on his shoulder. ''Go to sleep now. I'll see you in the morning.''

''Good to have you here, Sarah…appreciate…''

He heard the faint padding sound of her slippers as she made for the door. He heard the click of the door being closed.

And then he heard nothing else.

Sarah found it hard to get to sleep that night. Thoughts of the day's happenings kept rolling around in her head.

She still didn't know what had happened between Jed and Chance to cause their estrangement—and it was obvious Jed remembered nothing about it, either. What a mix-up.

And what a dilemma for him, to have lost his memory.

But, she acknowledged, it had changed things.

On first meeting the man, she'd taken an instant dislike to him. He'd been harsh, hostile, rude. But now, with his memory gone, he seemed a different person. And the main thing was, he'd shown no signs of wanting to kick her out. In fact, he'd said it was good to have her here.

She, of course, was interested in staying.

And naturally, he wouldn't try to kiss her again or invite her to share his bed. He'd made those advances only because he'd believed her to be his wife. Now that he knew she was not only his brother's widow but pregnant with his brother's child, he would, of course, keep his distance.

She wasn't about to tell him she'd kicked Chance out two years ago on account of his gambling. And she wasn't about to tell him that after Chance swore he'd reformed, she'd taken him back, but he'd gone on to break his promise.

The fact that she'd been a fool was nobody's business but her own.

Jed spent a restless night but around dawn finally fell into a deep sleep. When he awoke, it was almost ten o'clock, and judging by the sound of the rain blattering against the windowpanes, the stormy weather had returned.

He showered and dressed and made his way downstairs.

The house was quiet.

But as he walked along the corridor to the kitchen, he heard the voice of the weatherman on the radio.

"…and in the Whispering Mountain area, falling trees have resulted in electrical outages. Many rural homes are now without power. In addition, because of mud slides, several roads have been closed, including Route 1 through Raven Woods. By late afternoon, the rain will taper off…"

Jed pushed the door open and saw Sarah at the other side of the kitchen. She was standing by the wall phone with her back to him and she had the receiver at her ear. Before he could announce his presence, she dropped it back in place.

"Phoning somebody?" he asked.

She turned and ran a nervous hand through her long hair. She was wearing a shorty pink robe in a soft flannel fabric that clung to her figure, revealing the swell of her pregnancy. Her legs were long and shapely, and on her narrow feet she wore flat-heeled pink slippers with dainty pink bows. Her ankles were superb—

She cleared her throat and he flicked his gaze back to her face.

It was flushed. "The phone's out," she murmured. Tucking a sweep of hair behind her ear, she added, "I was checking as they said on the radio that lines were down in some areas."

She looked good enough to eat. Certainly good enough to kiss. His gaze zeroed in on her lips, which were cherry-pink and parted. He took a step forward.

She moved to stand behind a chair. Had she read his mind? Curving her fingers around the back of the chair, she threw him a wary look.

"Sorry about not being dressed yet," she said. "I slept in. I did peek in on you earlier to see if you wanted breakfast in bed but you looked so out of it I hated to disturb you. Are you ready to eat now?"

"I'm not that hungry. Maybe toast and coffee?"

"Sure. The children are in the sitting room. Why don't you join them and I'll bring the coffee through after I shower and get dressed?"

Sarah willed him to go. Even though he was at least twelve feet away, she could feel the effects of his animal magnetism. From the moment he'd come into the room, her nerve endings had been tingling. And the sexy way he'd looked at her mouth…it had made her feel hot and cold all over. A disturbing sensation and not one she welcomed.

"Sure," he said. "Will do."

After he left, her breath hissed out on a shiver. She'd never felt so uncomfortable around any man— and in that rugged black sweater and narrow-fitting jeans, he was sinfully attractive.…

But allowing herself to give in to the attraction she felt for him would be crazy under the circumstances. And determinedly dislodging his image from her mind, she put on the coffee and went upstairs to get dressed.

When she came down again, the coffee was ready. She made toast, buttered it and, after arranging everything on a tray, carried the tray to the sitting room.

Jed was stretched out on his back on a long sofa, his eyes closed. The children were sprawled on the hearth rug, Emma browsing through a picture book, Jamie fitting together the pieces of a wooden jigsaw puzzle. Jed looked as if he was dozing so she decided not to disturb him.

Moving forward, she deposited the tray quietly on an end table by the sofa.

Emma looked up and, after a glance at her uncle, whispered, ''What are you going to do now, Mom?''

''I'm going to sit here for a while.'' Sarah pulled over an ottoman. ''And work on the baby's jacket.''

''I's being quiet!'' Jamie said in a breathy whisper.

Smiling, Sarah ruffled his hair before unlooping her knitting bag from her arm and extricating the tiny white garment that she was knitting in bramble stitch.

For the next few minutes the only sounds in the room were the gentle hum of the gas fire, the crackle of pages turning, the snap of puzzle pieces being put in place, and the efficient click of Sarah's knitting needles. Outside, the wind still moaned, but it was abating.

Sarah paused as she felt the baby move. Fists poking? Knees jutting? Laying the knitting on her lap, she set her right hand over her belly.

''When's it due?''

She jerked her head up as the voice came from the sofa. Jed was looking at her, his eyes thoughtful.

''In about a month.''

''You don't show much.''

''No, I never do.''

''Boy or girl this time?''

''Don't know.''

''We didn't *want* to know, did we, Mom?'' Emma looked up from a picture of a witch on a broomstick.

''No, honey, we wanted it to be a surprise.''

Jamie crawled over to the sofa and pulled himself to his feet. "Hi, Unca Jed. You sleeping?"

"Not now, kid." Jed ruffled Jamie's blond hair. "How's the puzzle coming on?"

"I's almost finished."

"D'you wanna see my picture book, Uncle Jed?" Book open in her hands, Emma approached the sofa. "It doesn't have any words, but I can tell you what the story is."

"Honey, your uncle's tired—"

"It's okay, Sarah." His eyes met hers over Emma's head.

"At least have your coffee first."

"Mom, can I have some of Uncle Jed's toast?" Emma asked.

"Me, too!" Jamie said.

"Help yourselves," Jed said.

"Our daddy sold used cars," Emma said as she plucked a triangle of toast for herself and one for Jamie. "What do you do, Uncle Jed?"

"I don't know, Emma. This knock on the head— well, it's made me forget a lot of things." He glanced at Sarah. "I don't suppose you can help me out in that regard?"

"Sorry. I've no idea."

Emma and Jamie wandered over to the window, and Sarah poured a mug of coffee for Jed.

As he took it, he asked, "How come you didn't contact me right away after my brother died?"

"I didn't feel it was appropriate since Chance and you were estranged. But when Roberto Izzio tracked me down and started hounding me for the money Chance owed him—"

"Money? Chance left debts behind when he died?"

Sarah bit her lip. "Of course—you've forgotten. That's why I came here—to ask you for a loan." She looked away, embarrassed. Having to ask for help a second time was more than she had bargained for. "You apparently have the wherewithal because you did agree to—"

"Good, but the money's not important." His gesture was dismissive. "What *is* important is that you had to approach me when it's obviously the last thing you'd have chosen to do. You had nobody else to turn to?"

His concern brought a sting of tears to her eyes. She blinked them away as she shook her head.

"You don't have any family?"

"No one close," she said in a level tone. "No one I'd feel comfortable asking for that kind of help."

"So," he said musingly, "we're in the same boat. Both on our own." His smile was warm and genuine...and reassuring. "I'm glad you *did* find me, Sarah Morgan. You and I are family. And families should stick together."

Sarah forced an answering smile, but it didn't reach down inside her. He'd forgotten how harshly he'd treated her when she and the children had turned up at Morgan's Hope. He'd also forgotten how reluctant he'd been to let them stay over, even for one night. He'd hated her then and she didn't know why.

But whatever had happened between Jed and his brother had left Jed a bitter and angry man.

She felt her heart give a shiver of dread. At any moment, his memory might return.

What was going to happen then?

*   *   *

Jed dozed off after he'd finished his coffee, and when he awoke, he was alone in the room.

Levering himself up to a sitting position, he winced from the pain in his head—pain that intensified when questions started bombarding his brain. The uppermost one being: What did he do for a living?

Dammit, how he hated this not knowing!

Exasperation drove him to his feet and aimed him toward the door. The answer must be in the house somewhere.

As he left the room, from the kitchen drifted the babble of children's voices, accompanied by Sarah's laughter. The happy sounds tempted him to join them, but he resisted the impulse and circled the foyer, opening doors.

Behind the first was a powder room. Behind the second was a laundry room. Behind the third was a comfortably furnished den with an enormous TV set.

And behind the fourth was a study.

The room was paneled in dark wood and furnished with mahogany furniture. Undeniably a man's room. His room. Yet he had absolutely no memory of ever being in it before.

Through the window, which looked out on the back, he could see a large garden. And even taking into account that at this time of year most gardens weren't at their best, he could see that this garden showed years of neglect.

Frowning, he rounded his desk and sat on the swivel chair. He ran his fingers over the desk's smooth wood as his gaze flicked over the streamlined

IBM computer, the elegant gray printer, the black phone, the wire In basket.

Reaching for the mail in the In basket, he noted that the envelopes had already been slit. He scanned a hydro bill, a B.C. Tel bill, a cable TV bill. There was a postcard from Oslo from someone called Harry, who was "having a terrific time!"; and there was a receipt from the Salvation Army. And at the bottom of the pile, there was a letter.

He withdrew the crisp white page from the envelope.

The letterhead read: The Deborah Feigelman Art Gallery, 14A Merivale Square, Seattle.

He skimmed the computer-printed words.

Jed:
Firstly, please find enclosed A.D.'s check in the amount of $40,000 for *Phaedra*.
Secondly, re your decision not to attend the opening of our New York Feigelman Gallery in June, please reconsider. To have the reclusive Jed Morgan make an appearance would not only be a coup for me personally, it would bring added attention to your work, resulting in increased competition and even higher prices!

It was signed in green ink by Deborah herself.

So he was an artist. And much in demand apparently; which explained how he could afford to live the way he did.

He opened all the desk drawers in turn but found nothing to shed further light on his situation.

He got up and wandered around the room. The

bookcases were empty; the filing cabinet was empty. Feeling thwarted, he turned—to see Sarah watching him from the doorway.

"Hi," she said. "Trying to find out about yourself?"

He gestured toward the letter on his desk. "That's from a woman called Deborah Feigelman who has a gallery in Seattle. She sells my work. It appears I'm an artist."

"Yes." She smiled. "I know."

He raised his eyebrows.

"Those three oil paintings in the foyer," she said. "I was looking at them just now. Your signature's on them all. A bit of a scrawl, and Jed rather than Jedidiah, but the surname's unmistakably Morgan!"

He followed her to the foyer.

The paintings, which he'd paid little attention to before, were beautifully executed. He stared at the largest—a desert scene with zucchini-green cacti and lemon-yellow sand and a blinding white sky. He stared and waited. Hoping for a flash of memory.

Nothing.

He glanced wryly at Sarah. "It's like looking at the work of a stranger."

"A very talented stranger! But if you're an artist, you must have a studio! Let's see if we can find it."

They searched the house without success, ending up in the attic where their voices echoed hollowly.

"What I find strange," Jed said as he looked around the bare space, "is that there's no clutter. Anywhere."

"Maybe you're just a very tidy person."

"Or maybe I've just moved in!"

"No, this was where Chance said you lived."

They returned to the main floor and made their way to the kitchen, where Jamie and Emma sat at the table molding figures from Play-Doh.

Emma slid from her chair. "I'm finished, Mom."

"I's finished, too!" Jamie clambered down off his seat.

"Do you have a TV, Uncle Jed?" Emma dragged Girl off the table and, in a practised move, maneuevred her thumb into her mouth while clutching the doll's neck with all four fingers.

Jed picked up the figure she'd been working on.

"Hey," he said, "this is terrific."

Emma raised her gray eyes to him. "It's an elephant."

"Yeah, I can see that. Sarah, your daughter has a real knack for modeling. You've done a great job, kid!"

Emma slid her wet thumb from her mouth. "Mrs. Melton always gives me an A for art." Her brow puckered in an impatient frown. "When am I going back to school, Mom?"

"Soon," Sarah said with a vague gesture.

"But, Mom—"

"We'll talk about it later, honey. In the meantime, I'm going to make lunch for your uncle."

"Unca Jed." Jamie tugged his sleeve. "Is there a TV in the house?"

"Yup."

"Oh, goody." Distracted, Emma dragged him to the door. "C'mon, Uncle Jed. Show us where it is."

When he came back a few minutes later, Sarah was ladling potato soup into a blue bowl.

"What are they watching?" she asked as he sat down.

"A Disney movie. They just caught the beginning."

Sarah set the bowl in front of him and then popped a couple of tomato and cheese buns into the toaster oven. Glancing out the window, she noticed that the rain had slackened off to a drizzle.

"Sarah…"

She turned as Jed addressed her.

"…you seemed evasive when Emma asked about going back to school. Is there a problem?"

"No, it's just that I'm not too sure of my plans at present." She tried to sound casual.

"Because you've stayed to look after me? Hell, you don't have to hang on here now—I'm perfectly able to look after myself. You have your own life to live. Aren't you in a hurry to get back to your own place—especially with your being pregnant?"

She hesitated before saying, "I don't have a place right now. I had a basement apartment, but it went with my job, and I lost the job earlier this week."

"You were still working?" He frowned. "This far on in your pregnancy?"

"It was nothing too onerous. I was baby-sitting for friends—a young professional couple. They gave me the use of their basement suite in exchange for looking after their three-year-old while they were at work. They'd promised me I'd keep the job after my baby was born, but out of the blue the husband got a plum posting to New York, so they upped and left."

"And left *you* high and dry." He shook his head. "What a shock that must have been, to be out on the street, no job, no place to call home—especially in your condition. Well, you can stay on at Morgan's Hope for a while. I'm not suggesting you stay permanently—you'd probably go crazy stuck up here, seeing nobody for weeks on end. But for the short term, could you hack it? At least till after the baby's born and you get your strength back.''

Could she hack it? Sarah felt a lump in her throat. Oh, yes, she could hack it all right! But what would happen if Jed's memory returned? She cringed inside at the thought of being subjected to his anger and hostility again.

''It's kind of you,'' she said, ''but...I'll move on as soon as you're feeling better. I have a good friend I can stay with in Vancouver till after the baby's born.'' She flushed as the fib popped out smoothly. ''And of course you're right...I'd *never* settle to country life.''

By the time she'd finished speaking, her cheeks were burning. How she hated lying. She had to get away from him before she got even more deeply involved in her deception.

Rising from her chair, she said, ''I'd like to go for a walk, get some fresh air. Would you mind keeping an eye on the children for a bit?''

CHAPTER FIVE

JED watched from the den window as Sarah crossed the forecourt.

She walked slowly, her hands stuffed into the pockets of her anorak, her face lifted to the drizzle as if she were savoring the coolness on her heated skin.

Because her skin *had* been heated, he mused as he watched her disappear from view. When she'd turned down his invitation to stay on at Morgan's Hope, her cheeks had become as scarlet as that anorak she was wearing. And she'd looked guilty as hell. But guilty of what?

"Uncle Jed." Emma snuggled past him and stood with her palms on the windowsill as she gazed out. "Where's my mom?"

"She's gone for a walk, honeybunch."

"She likes to walk," Emma said. "On Mirren Street up in Quesnel where we lived, we had a park close by, and me and Mom and Jamie used to walk there a lot. Then—" her voice became pensive "—Daddy came back to live with us again, and when she got sick because a baby was coming she didn't feel like walking for the longest while."

"Why did your daddy go away?" Jed asked. "Did he have a job somewhere else?"

"He went away because of the horsies."

"The...horsies?"

Emma nodded emphatically. "He liked the horsies.

And—'' she gave him a meaningful look ''—he spent all our money on them. That's why Mom got mad at him and told him she didn't want to be married to him anymore.''

Jed cursed silently. He'd walked into something without realizing it…and he wanted to get out. Fast. Eliciting information from a child this way was not his style. "Emma, how about you get one of your books and—"

"Daddy *promised*." Emma looked up at him soulfully. "He *promised* he'd be good this time and that's why Mom let him come back. But he wasn't." She turned and looked out the window again. "He broke his promise. And that made my mom cry. A lot." Her breath made mist on the windowpane and she started drawing with the tip of a thin index finger.

A round face. With a sad, down-turned mouth.

Jed compressed his lips. So…the debts his brother had run up had been gambling debts. And his marriage to Sarah had been a troubled one because of his obsession.

"Honey—" he turned Emma gently by the shoulder "—if you've finished watching TV, why don't you get one of your books and I'll read you and Jamie a story?"

They crossed to the hearth where Jamie was playing with two Tonka trucks. Jed took a seat on the long sofa and said to him, "Hey, kid, come sit up here with me."

As Jamie scrambled happily up beside his uncle, Emma picked through her books and finally selected one. She set the chosen book on his knee before clambering up to sit by him on the other side.

"This is our favorite," she confided. "*Goldilocks and the Three Bears*." She cuddled close and looked up at him expectantly.

Jed opened the book at the first page. "'Once upon a time…'"

Sarah walked for about fifteen minutes before she turned and started back up the mountain track. The drizzle had thinned to a fine mist. She relished its coolness, just as she relished the rain-washed, pine-scented air.

What an exquisite spot this was.

Deep inside her, she felt an ache of intense longing. How simple life would be up here, how simple and how beautiful.

And how she had lied when she told Jed she could never settle to life in the country. She loved the country. And she found Whispering Mountain absolutely enchanting.

Morgan's Hope was a perfect place to bring up a family. A perfect place for children—

She felt the baby move: that odd, fluid shifting of bone and flesh. Of this world but not yet in this world.

A miracle in the making.

Wonderment and a rush of euphoria drove away her wistfulness and added a buoyant lift to her step as she made her way back to the house.

After taking off her shoes and jacket, she crossed the foyer and pushed open the door to the den. What she saw made her smile.

Jed was lying asleep on a sofa, and curled up beside him, also asleep, were the children.

Sarah leaned against the doorjamb, her gaze on Jed.

Even in sleep, his face was stronger than Chance's had been. And even in sleep, lines remained etched around his eyes, between his brows, bracketing his mouth. Lines that gave his face character. Lines that had been missing from his brother's face.

Chance had shaken off responsibility the way Max shook off raindrops.

Sarah expelled a sigh, and as the sound whispered into the room, Jed's eyes opened and met hers.

For a moment, his expression was blank. Then he shifted his gaze to the children lying trustingly curled against him, and Sarah saw his mouth quirk in a smile.

He eased himself off the sofa and walked over to her.

"Was the road okay?" he asked in a low voice.

"Almost washed out at one point, but now that the rain has abated, I guess the danger's past." She frowned as she scrutinized him. "You're looking pretty washed out yourself. I think you should go back to bed."

"Sarah, your daughter was talking about her father…"

She stiffened. "What did she say?"

"Enough for me to deduce that Chance's debts were gambling ones. Am I right?"

"Yes."

"And his gambling caused problems in your marriage?"

"Emma told you that?"

"Not in so many words, but that was the gist of it. She said you'd kicked Chance out but had then taken him back—"

"I'd appreciate," she said tersely, "if you'd refrain from quizzing my daughter when I'm not around."

"I wasn't prying." His tone was level. "Emma volunteered the information."

"While holding you down, of course, and forcing you to listen!" Her laugh had a tinge of scorn.

"I tried to stop her," he said wearily, "but she just drove on. If you must know, I can do without hearing this kind of information right now—it's not a barrel of laughs, discovering that one's brother was an irresponsible b—"

"Mom?" Emma's sleepy voice came from the sofa. "How come you and Daddy are fighting again?"

Sarah flashed Jed a tight glance and then brushed past him. Emma had struggled up to a sitting position and she pushed her hair back from her face as her mother approached.

"I'm talking to your uncle Jed." Sarah sat on the edge of the sofa and drew Emma into her arms. "We weren't fighting, sweetie. We were just discussing something."

Emma peered past her. "Oh. Uncle Jed." She blinked and came fully awake. "Where are you going?"

"I'm going upstairs to lie down for a while."

Sarah turned to look at him. She felt a stab of concern when she saw how white his face was, and her anger dissipated in a flash. "Can I bring you something? A cup of tea?"

"No thanks. But there is one thing you can do for me. Tomorrow, if the phone lines are still down, would you let me use your car? I want to go into town, make a few calls. Try to find out more about my situation.''

''I'll drive you. And only if you're well enough to go out.'' When he made to protest, she added firmly, ''It's my car, Jed. And those are my terms.''

Jed didn't reappear till after Sarah had put the children to bed for the night. She was in the kitchen, wondering when he was going to wake up and come downstairs, when she heard his step in the corridor.

''You're looking a lot better,'' she said when he walked into the room. ''How do you feel?''

''More like myself,'' he said. ''Whoever myself is!'' he added with a grin. ''Is the phone working yet?''

''No.''

''Have you eaten dinner?''

''Yes, we ate around six, but—'' She broke off as she heard a yelp outside the back door. ''Max. I'll let him in.''

The dog headed straight for his dish, where Sarah had tossed a couple of doggy bones. As she closed the door, she heard Jed say, ''Where did these come from?''

He'd picked up the two envelopes she'd arranged on the island earlier. When she'd let Max out, she'd noticed the letter box outside and, on checking it, had found the two items of mail. Both were addressed to J. C. Morgan. One was a personal letter from a B. Tierney; the second was from a Vancouver furniture store.

''They were in the mailbox,'' she said.

He scrutinized the second envelope before slitting

it open and extricating the invoice it contained. He whistled as he looked at it. "Looks as if I went on a major shopping spree. It would seem as if every stick of furniture in this house was purchased in one fell swoop just a month ago."

"That explains why the place has such a fresh, un-lived-in feel," Sarah said. "Everything's new."

He opened the first envelope. From it he took a flimsy sheet of pink paper, and from where she was standing, Sarah could see a spidery, feminine scrawl.

Jed raised his eyebrows as he scanned the message, and when he finally looked up, his expression was strained.

"This is from someone called Brianna. Apparently, the lady and I have known each other for many years. She mentions attending my wedding—to her sister, Jeralyn."

"You're...married? But—"

"But if I am, where's my wife? A good question!"

Sarah couldn't understand why the thought of his being married made her feel so flat. "Tomorrow," she said, managing an upbeat tone, "you'll surely get some answers."

"This woman says..." Jed held out the letter. "Here."

After a moment's hesitation, Sarah took it and began reading.

Jed, I hope you're enjoying your new home after the years of "camping out"! Thanks again for hiring me as your interior decorator and for giving me carte blanche—a decorator's dream! It's going to be up to you to give it a lived-in look and I shall expect, by our next visit, that you'll have done just that. You'll have noticed by now that I stocked your freezer and left oodles of food in the fridge. It'll be up to you, also, to hire a gardener and get Jeralyn's garden licked into shape again!

On our way back from the "new" Morgan's Hope, the children and I dropped by to visit Nick and Allie Campbell, and spent the weekend at their ranch. The countryside was at its best, and I found myself thinking, as I so often do, about you and Jeralyn. It's such a lovely time of year—Jer's favorite. She did love Spring! Remember how she planned your wedding for April so she could have masses of bluebells in church?

Harry phoned last night from Europe. He said he'd sent you a PC—he seems to be enjoying the conference.

Your affectionate sister-in-law,
Brianna

Sarah handed back the letter. "She sounds nice. And she does answer some more questions. You should get in touch with her—she'll surely be able to help fill in other blanks in your memory."

Jed set the letter on the counter. "I wonder if I'm divorced? Must be either that or—"

"Or you may be widowed." Sarah sighed. "This must be incredibly frustrating for you."

"I wonder what Brianna meant by 'camping out?' Sounds as if I must have been roughing it…and for quite a while."

"Brianna referred to the "new" Morgan's Hope.

Do you think she meant that literally—that the house itself was new?''

''More likely that it's been rebuilt. The garden's totally neglected, but I noticed that the shrubs and trees are well established.'' He paused as he saw Sarah rub a hand absently over the small of her back. ''Are you okay?''

''Just feeling a bit draggy. Maybe I walked farther down the mountain than I should have. I like walking, but I'm used to the flat.''

''Probably the drive down from Quesnel's catching up with you, too. Go through to the den and put your feet up. I'll bring you something…a mug of hot milk?''

His kindness touched her. She could get used to this, having someone to look after her. But she mustn't get used to it; it wasn't going to last. ''I have to heat your dinner—I made a quiche. If you'll give me a minute to—''

''Go!''

She took one look at the implacable glint in his eyes…and she went.

Jed busied himself, heating a mug of milk, warming up a slice of quiche. As he waited for the microwave to stop humming, he noticed a calendar on the wall. Walking over to inspect the single notation on it, he raised his eyebrows when he read it. Apparently, someone called Minerva was leaving on the last day of the month. Leaving here? Or leaving somewhere else to come here?

Ah, well, time would tell….

The microwave beeped, and he turned away from

the calendar. After setting his dinner and Sarah's milk on a tray, he ambled through to the den.

He paused in the doorway. Sarah was lying back on one of the corduroy recliners, her eyes closed.

She looked so young. She must have been a teenager when she gave birth to her first child—little more than a child herself then. Now she had two with a third on the way. Quite a burden for a single mom to carry on her own.

But she wasn't on her own now. She had him. And he was going to give her all the support she needed. Apart from the fact that she was family, he enjoyed having her around.

She must have sensed his presence because she opened her eyes. ''Oh, hi,'' she said, and awkwardly shifted to a sitting position as he set his tray on the coffee table.

''What's the date?'' he asked.

When she told him, he said with a self-deprecatory grin, ''That means Minerva will be leaving next week.''

''Ah, the mysterious Minerva.'' She chuckled. ''I guess you don't know who she is?''

''Haven't a clue.'' He handed over her mug.

As Sarah sipped her drink and he dug into his ham and egg quiche, the silence that ensued was companionable.

When he was finished, he said, ''That was fantastic. Where did you learn to cook?''

Sarah hesitated for a beat and then said, ''At home.''

''Your mother taught you?''

''My mother didn't cook. My father died when I

was eight and after that she worked full-time, so we had a housekeeper. Mariah enjoyed having me help her in the kitchen…and I just picked things up as we went along.''

Sarah didn't add that her mother would have had a fit if she'd known Sarah was hanging around with one of the servants. Deirdre Hallston was a snob of the highest order and she did *not* believe in mixing with the hired help.

''Your mother was a career woman?''

''Is. She's still alive, still works full-time.''

''What does she do?''

''She has an administrative position with one of the top electronics companies in Vancouver.'' Sarah wasn't about to tell him that her father had founded the wildly successful company, JD Electronics, and after his death her mother had taken it over. Deirdre Hallston was now one of the wealthiest women on the West Coast.

''I don't mean to pry,'' Jed said, ''but…with your baby so close to being born, surely the place to be would be with your mother?''

Sarah felt her nerves tighten as bad memories flooded her mind. ''My mother disowned me when I married Chance.''

''Disowned you?'' He frowned. ''What the hell did she do—give you a 'him or me' choice?''

''More or less. Except it was no choice. I was in love with Chance. And besides—'' she toyed with her wedding ring ''—I was pregnant.''

He whistled under his breath. ''So…how old were you?''

''Just turned eighteen.''

"And my brother?"

"Chance was almost twenty-four."

"Dammit, you were just a kid—he should have been tarred and feathered for taking advantage of you! Were you still at school?"

"In my final year. But you can't put all the blame on Chance. It takes two to—"

"You're an only child?"

"Yes."

"I can see why your mother would have been shattered. What a disappointment that must have been. I'm sure she had high hopes for you—"

"You sound just like her!" Sarah lumbered to her feet and glared at him, her eyes sparking. "If that's the kind of superior attitude you had toward Chance, it's no wonder the two of you fell out!"

Jed pushed himself up from his chair and pinned her with a steady gaze. "I have no idea why my brother and I fell out. And we're not talking about Chance and me—we're talking about you and your mother. All I'm saying is, wouldn't it have made more sense to go to your mother when things got so rough for you? Does she have room for you? You and the kids?"

"Yes." Sarah's tone was stiff. "She has room."

"Her attitude may have mellowed. People do change, Sarah."

Her mother would never change, Sarah thought with a feeling of deep sadness as she recalled the distant expression on her mother's face when she'd said to Sarah, "From now on, you are no longer welcome in this house." Deirdre Hallston had a block of ice where her heart should be. "My mother's the last person in the world I'd turn to for help. Now if you'll excuse me, I'm tired and I'm going to bed."

She scooped up her empty mug and made to brush past Jed, but he caught her arm. "Just a minute."

She tried to wriggle free, but he tightened his grip.

"I don't want to fight," he said. "In your condition, it's not good for you to get upset."

When he looked at her like that, concern darkening his green eyes, she felt her resistance melt.

"I'm sorry," she murmured. "I don't want to fight, either. I guess what you said struck a nerve."

"I didn't mean to sound critical, but I couldn't help seeing the situation objectively. A parent wants what's best for his or her child—"

"I was eighteen!" she protested. "Old enough to—"

He pressed two fingers over her mouth. And grinned. "Hey," he drawled, "this is where we came in."

Her eyes were huge. She raised a hand to tug away his fingers, but he flicked them around and caught her wrist. He felt the fast *throb-throb* of her pulse against his skin.

He should have released her then but didn't. Couldn't. She was so feminine, so soft, so lovely. His gaze slid from her startled gray eyes to her soft, parted lips.

The air between them tightened.

Her breathing quickened.

His decision to kiss her arose at the exact same moment she swayed toward him. And as he claimed her lips, he heard the faintest whimper deep in her throat.

He cupped her head in his hands, then sifted his fingers down through her hair. He felt the glossy strands fall like sunlight to her shoulders.

Their lips clung. And searched. And clung. And lingered. She tasted ineffably sweet. Of honey. Manna. Heaven. She leaned into him...

And he felt the hard pressure of her belly.

The pressure of his brother's child.

The thought was like being doused with icy water. *What was he doing*? In an abrupt move, he released her, appalled that he'd acted so carelessly, succumbing to temptation and thinking only of himself. Chance had taken advantage of her when she was just a teenager, a teenager probably desperate for love since she'd apparently had none at home. Would he be any better than his brother if he took advantage of her now, while she was a guest under his roof and pregnant to boot?

Angry with himself, he stepped back, his face darkened in a scowl.

Her expression couldn't have been more wounded if he'd slapped her. He cursed silently as he realized she must be assuming his anger was directed at her.

"I'm sorry." His tone was harsh. "That was a mistake. It won't happen again. I promise you."

Her eyes clouded over. "As I said a moment ago—" she inhaled a shaky breath "—it takes two."

She turned from him and, hardly knowing what she was doing, walked out of the room. Heading for the kitchen on wobbly legs, she put a hand to her cheek. It was burning hot. She touched her lips. Her mouth still retained the imprint of his lips.

She winced as she recalled their kiss; groaned as

she recalled how she'd so eagerly given herself to it. He'd been just as eager…till he'd felt the baby butt into him.

She could well imagine the cold reality that had jolted him then. He had wasted no time in pushing her away.

It was obvious that though he might find her kissable, he wasn't interested in getting involved with her. And who could blame him? What man would want to take on a whole new family, including a child yet to be born?

Certainly not Jedidiah Morgan. She recalled his icy response the night she arrived, when he learned she had Jamie and Emma with her. He'd made it clear that he couldn't get rid of the three of them fast enough.

She deeply regretted that she'd talked him into letting them stay that first night at Morgan's Hope. If she'd left when he'd ordered her out, she wouldn't be in the impossible position she found herself in now.

"Hi, kids." Jed greeted Emma and Jamie with a smile as he entered the kitchen next morning. They were seated at the table, scoffing cereal from yellow bowls. "How's it going?"

"Unca Jed!" Jamie said gleefully. "Good morning."

"You slept really late," Emma said in a faintly superior tone. "We've been up for *ages*!"

"Where's your mom?"

Emma waved her cereal spoon in the direction of the back door. "She's outside with Max."

Jed strolled out the back door into a day that was

bright and breezy, with white clouds scudding across a china-blue sky. Sarah was nowhere to be seen, but he heard Max barking around at the front. He followed the sound.

Sarah was standing in the forecourt, throwing a ball for Max. Her blond hair flew about in the wind while the hem of her navy-and-white-striped shirt flapped around her thighs. Her legs looked endlessly long in a pair of narrow-fitting blue jeans, and her casual stance was as elegant as any model's.

Jed heard her easy laugh gurgle out delightedly as Max chased after the ball.

He smiled as he came up behind her.

"Hi," he said. "Good morning."

She spun around, her expression startled. "Heavens, don't *do* that!" She pressed a hand to her breastbone. "You could have given me a heart attack!"

As their eyes met, a powerful jolt set his own heart reeling. He stared at her while the dizzying current sizzled through him. Not just an electrical current caused by physical attraction—though that was part of it. There was something more. An emotional connection. And one so intense it stole his breath away.

She'd felt it, too.

He could tell by the flush of her cheeks, the dilation of her pupils, the rounding of her lips in a silent *Oh*!

"Sarah." His voice was husky. "I—"

Max bounded between them, almost knocking Sarah over as he thrust his nose up at her, the ball gritted in his teeth. Jed saw her swallow hard, then she laughed as she tugged the ball from Max—but it was a nervous sound unlike the easy laugh that had rippled from her earlier.

"Good dog." She tossed the ball again, and as it rolled away down the drive, Max bounded after it. Lightly, she said to Jed, "I'll come in now and make your breakfast."

The moment was past, the connection broken. Thanks to Max. Why the hell did he have to come back right then?

The connection was broken, but the tension between them remained. He heard it in Sarah's voice as she said on their way to the back door, "Do you still want to go into town this morning?"

"Yup. Will you let me have the car?"

"No, I'll drive you. I have a bit of shopping to do anyway. But you do look a lot better this morning."

"Yeah, feel better, too. Okay, then, we'll all go. And once we get there, we can split up for a while. You can do whatever you have to do, and I'll find a phone. Do you have Izzio's number?"

"I have the number for his cell phone."

"Good. You give me that and the other particulars, and I'll get in touch, find out where he wants me to send the money. Then I want to call my agent and of course I want to call Brianna. I need to know about Jeralyn—and I'm curious to find out why Chance and I became estranged. If anybody can answer my questions, it will surely be Brianna."

He thought he saw a flicker of anxiety in Sarah's eyes, but a second later she moved in front of him as they entered the kitchen, so he couldn't be sure.

He decided he must have imagined it. After all, she'd shown a keen interest in finding out who he was—wasn't she the one who'd suggested searching the house for his studio? And when she'd read

Brianna's letter, she'd wasted no time in advising him to get in touch with his sister-in-law.

What he'd interpreted as anxiety had probably been anticipation. The same kind of anticipation he himself was feeling. He couldn't wait to get to town. He couldn't wait to get the answers to all his pressing questions.

CHAPTER SIX

"JED!" Deborah Feigelman's contralto voice flowed along the telephone line like melted chocolate. "You got my letter? You've changed your mind, you're going to come after all?"

Jed stood with his back to the food fair in the mall, trying to ignore the hubbub behind him. "Deborah, I'm thinking it over." He injected a rueful smile into his tone. "Remind me again why I decided not to attend!" Dammit, why couldn't he come up with the truth? That he just couldn't remember! But no, he still felt that was a weakness and one to which he wasn't about to admit.

"Jed!" The agent's tone was reproachful. "As if you need reminding! You've been a recluse for more than six years, ever since Jeralyn died—"

Jed felt the day had suddenly become darker. So his wife was dead. Though he'd suspected this might be the case, it didn't make the news any easier to take. Didn't protect him from the explosion of shock. And added to the shock was sorrow. Sorrow that he couldn't remember her.

"—but it's time to move on. Move on and start over. Lord knows we all miss Jer, but she'd be the last person to want you to become a hermit. You will come, won't you, darling?"

"Deborah, about *Phaedra*—"

"Ari Demetri is thrilled with it. I'm going to for-

ward a photograph he sent me—he's placed it in his
atrium. By far the most magnificent sculpture you've
done!''

He was a sculptor?

Jed spread out a hand, examined the callused
palm....

''Darling, I have to go. I'm closing the gallery
early. I have an important appointment. But I appreciate your call and I sense a teensy crack in your
armor. I'm going to keep working on it. Just one last
thing. Mitch will be coming next week to pick up
Minerva as arranged—''

''Deborah—''

''Sorry, Jed. I really have to go. Talk to you soon.''

And with that, the line went dead.

Cursing under his breath, he called the gallery
again, but this time there was no answer. The phone
just rang, and rang, and rang.

Bursting with frustration, he slumped against the
wall, oblivious to the noise behind him as he mulled
over the little he had learned.

He'd expected Brianna would be the one to satisfy
his curiosity about himself and his past, but when
he'd called Information, he'd found his sister-in-law
had an unlisted number and no way was the operator
going to divulge it.

Deborah had given him some answers, but not
enough. He still didn't know why he and Chance had
fallen out.

On the plus side, he'd gotten in touch with Izzio,
no problem. And he'd also managed to locate the
bank branch where he conducted his financial busi-

ness and had a talk with the manager, a middle-aged man called John Kincaid.

He had asked Kincaid to make out a certified check in the name of Roberto Izzio, then arranged to have him forward the check to the address Izzio had given him.

"Your balance took a bit of a knock when you paid the builder," Kincaid had said after he'd checked the status of his account. "But you're still in the black." He shoved a statement across his desk.

Jed's mind had boggled when he saw what he was worth.

It had still been boggling when he left the bank and crossed the street to the mall to make his phone calls. Now, after his talk with Deborah, his mind was focused elsewhere.

Abstractedly, he walked out of the mall. He was supposed to meet Sarah in the parking lot at noon. He was early. And when he glanced around and noticed a church steeple a block or two away, a thought occurred to him. With determined steps, he set off in that direction.

When he got there, he found what he'd half expected—right next to the church was a cemetery.

He pushed open the wrought-iron gate and made his way along the first of many narrow paths, searching for a grave with his wife's name on the headstone. He knew it was a shot in the dark, but it was worth a try.

He'd covered about two-thirds of the area with no success when a man approached, his gray hair untidy as a bird's nest, his wiry body bent.

''Looking for somebody?'' he asked Jed bluntly.
''I'm the caretaker of this here place.''

''Oh, hi. Yes, I'm looking for…Jeralyn Morgan.''

''Ah, the painter lady. Died in a fire some years back. The smoke inhalation's what got to her, so I hear'd.''

Jed clenched his fists. He'd barely had time to assimilate the news that his wife was no longer alive and now he had to cope with this—

''You won't find her in this cemetery, laddie.'' The man shuffled around and pointed with a gnarled finger. ''The way I hear'd it, her hubby scattered her ashes up there on Whispering Mountain.''

Surely *this* was something a man would— should!—remember. Jed forced himself to focus, willing his memory to stir as he focused on this information.

But…to no avail.

Disappointment spiraled sourly through him.

''Built a new house on the old site,'' the caretaker went on. ''Or so I hear'd. But keeps to himself. Gone barmy, folks say.'' Muttering to himself, he shambled away. ''Leastways, that's what I hear'd.''

Jed made his way slowly back to the parking lot. It was incredible that such a tragedy could have been wiped from his memory. A tragedy that had apparently left him so devastated with grief that people thought him crazy.

According to that old fellow, he'd become a recluse.

Well, the onset of his amnesia had obviously caused a sea of change in him. He was no longer a recluse. No longer wanted to be one. He *enjoyed* having Sarah and the children at Morgan's Hope.

And he was specially thankful to have her in his life today so he could tell her about Jeralyn. He knew she'd offer sympathy and comfort, and right now, he needed both.

"There you are." The drugstore cashier shoved Sarah's purchase across the counter. "Haven't seen you around here before. You on holiday in the area?"

"Mmm." The store wasn't busy and Sarah sensed that the bosomy brunette was in the mood to chat. She, however, was not. Briskly, she tucked the vitamins into her purse.

"Nice little kids you got there." The cashier nodded her approval. "Well behaved."

Sarah glanced at Emma and Jamie, who had drifted over to a magazine rack. "Yes, they—" She broke off at the sight of a framed print on the wall above the rack. The picture looked familiar, and in a flash she realized why. The original painting hung in Jed's foyer.

"That's Lake Moresby, far end of town." The cashier had obviously noticed her interest. "Stunning, isn't it?"

"Mmm, it is."

"She was a local, her that done it. Married to that sculptor fella Morgan, up on Whispering Mountain."

So Jed was a sculptor. Was it possible his studio was on the grounds of Morgan's Hope—tucked away in the forest?

"That poor man." The brunette's kohl-lined eyes had taken on a gossipy gleam. "What a tragedy. Lost his wife when his house went afire. He was in his studio at the time…late at night…never knew a thing till it was too late.''

Sarah stifled a sound of dismay. What a tragedy indeed. And Jed…had he by now learned of it from Brianna? She herself didn't want to glean information from this stranger; didn't want to listen to any more.

''Well,'' she said crisply, ''I'll be getting along—''

''Married eleven years they were—and boy, she was a looker, with scarlet-painted lips and glossy black hair curlin' right to her butt. Always dressed in them long traily skirts and decked herself out with fancy beads and baubles. Bo-he-mian, some folks called her. But not an air or grace about her, for all that she was such a beauty! And her hubby—well, Jedidiah Morgan's always been well-thought-of around here. But that brother of his…he never showed his face again—'' the woman had lowered her voice to a confidential whisper ''—*after the fire.*''

Sarah had been anxious to break away, but at the mention of Chance she stiffened. What did he have to do with this? Despite herself, she waited for the other woman to go on.

The cashier leaned forward. ''It was all hushed up, but everybody knew 'twas him that set the place alight. Fire started in the basement, ciggy in the sofa—and him the only smoker in the house. Well, he got out but never managed to save his sister-in-law. And he hightailed it out of the county so fast—well, it was all hushed up like I said, but it was him all right that was at the root of it.''

Chance was responsible for the tragedy in Jed's past? Sarah placed a steadying hand on the counter as nausea swept through her. During their marriage, she'd found out that her husband was irresponsible, but she'd never in her worst nightmares guessed he'd harbored such a terrible secret.

The woman was still talking, but Sarah was no longer listening. With a distracted "Excuse me", she stepped away. "Emma." Her voice shook. "Take Jamie's hand, honey. Let's go."

"You take care now," the clerk called after her. "And have a good day!"

The words echoed in Sarah's head as she walked out of the store. Have a good day. As if that were possible, given what she'd just found out.

While she'd been in the mall, dark clouds had moved in from the west, blotting out the sun. But she was barely aware of the change in the weather. With her mind in a turmoil, she tucked the children into the Cutlass. She understood now why Jed had turned on her so savagely when he'd found out who she was. He must have hated Chance for causing the fatal fire; must still hate him…and everyone connected with him.

Despair overwhelmed her as the full impact of what this meant sank in. It would be *unthinkable* to stay on at Morgan's Hope for even one more night. She had to leave.

And leave today.

But first she had to tell Jed what she'd found out— her conscience wouldn't let her do otherwise.

Her very soul cringed at the prospect.

She glanced at her watch. They'd arranged to meet at noon. She was a few minutes early.

With her fingers curled around the handle of the

driver's door, she turned and scanned the parking lot.
Her heartbeats faltered when she saw Jed striding toward her. And her heart plunged when she saw the
dark expression on his face. If she'd hoped his mis-
sion would be unsuccessful, she was out of luck.
Judging by the grim set of his jaw, he'd reached
Brianna and she'd told him everything.

Please, she prayed, let him not blow up at me in
front of the children.

She stepped quickly toward him so they couldn't
hear what she was going to say.

"Jed, I know we have to talk, but please—can it
wait till we get back to Morgan's Hope?"

"Of course. This is neither the time nor the
place—" He broke off abruptly as a peal of thunder
cracked overhead. "Let's get going," he said
brusquely. "There's a storm on the way. And give
me the keys," he added as he propelled her back to
the car. "You look all in. I'll drive home."

She opened her mouth to protest, but when she saw
the implacable glint in his eyes, she handed him the
keys without another a word.

Jed strained to see through the pewter-gray sheet of
water lashing the windshield as he maneuvered the
Cutlass up the mountain track. The heavens had
opened as they left town, and the dirt track was dan-
gerously slick with mud.

He threw Sarah a sideways glance. Her body was
rigid, her gaze glued ahead. Dammit, he thought irritably, where had this storm sprung from? Anxiety
was the last thing she needed in her delicate condition.

Not too far to go now, though.

Focusing again on the road, he almost didn't notice the turbulent waters of a narrow creek to the left. When he did, he drew his breath in sharply. Overflowing its banks, the water hurtled down the mountain toward the track, diverted only at the last moment by a wall of rocks that had obviously been built there to prevent the road being washed out by heavy rains. Water already sluiced ominously over the rocks and gushed over the track in a swirling stream.

This was going to be nasty.

Grasping the steering wheel more tightly, he jammed his foot down on the accelerator, but at that very instant he was appalled to see the creek waters demolish the rock barrier and flood over the track, directly in their path.

"Jed!" Sarah's voice was high with alarm. "Look—"

"Hang tight!" The tires dragged as he drove the car into the waters, the vehicle bucking as he plowed on over the rutted track. "We'll make it!" He sent up a silent prayer that he could keep his promise.

Vaguely, he heard Emma cry, "What's happening?" Then all his attention was concentrated on getting the car through the treacherous waters; struggling to keep it going uphill despite the powerful current that threatened to sweep the vehicle into the ditch.

He held his breath, fought to keep control of the vehicle, felt a surge of panic as he seemed to be losing the battle…

And then it was over.

Hallelujah, they were through it.

"Sarah—" his voice was rough "—are you okay?"

She expelled a shaky breath and sank back. "Yes, I'm fine."

Emma unclicked her seat belt and clambered around so she could peer out the rear window.

"Holy moly," she cried, "the whole road's washed away!"

Jed flashed a look in his rearview mirror…and barely managed to suppress an oath as he caught a rain-swept glimpse of uprooted shrubs and debris and rocks whirling across the track. They'd got through just in the nick of time.

And dammit, they'd all be stranded at Morgan's Hope till the floods receded and the track could be repaired.

But his uppermost feeling was one of relief. He carried a precious cargo in this old car; he'd never have forgiven himself if Sarah or the children had come to harm while in his care.

He glanced again at Sarah and noticed, with a sense of unease, that her face was ashen. When they'd met up in the parking lot earlier, he'd thought that she looked pale and strained. She looked a helluva lot worse now.

He decided to shelve his plan to fill her in on everything he'd learned about Jeralyn; the details could wait. He'd tell her that he was a widower, but he wouldn't tell her the circumstances of his wife's death. That would distress her and she'd already been through enough today.

He wanted to protect her.

As that thought filtered into his mind, he realized

how much his sister-in-law had come to mean to him in the few short days since she'd walked into his life.

"Is it time for lunch?" Emma piped up. "I'm hungry."

"Yup," he said. "It's that time. And I'm going to do the cooking while your mom puts her feet up."

"Uncle Jed," Emma said as she swallowed the last morsel of her bun, "that was the most delicious burger I ever tasted!"

"I second that," Sarah murmured.

"Where did you learn to cook, Uncle Jed?" Emma cocked her head to one side as she looked at him.

"My mom and dad had a restaurant. He was a chef—" Jed gave a low whistle. "How the heck did I know that when my past is such a blank? I guess I must have helped out in the kitchen when I was a kid, got the basics." His smile was wry. "Like riding a bike, maybe cooking's something you never forget—even if you can't remember your own name!"

"Did you really forget your own name?" Emma wrinkled her nose.

"Sure did—and a whole lot of other stuff, too!"

"You said you were going to make phone calls in town and find out about yourself. Did you do that, Uncle Jed? What did you find out?"

Sarah felt a quiver of panic. She rose from the table.

"Excuse me," she said. "I'm going to take Jamie upstairs to bed. He's dropping off." And that was no lie; his eyes were heavy, his eyelids drooping. She slid him down from his booster seat and he made no protest. "Emma, you come upstairs, too."

"I don't want a nap!" Emma pouted.

"You don't have to. You can lie on my bed and read the comics we bought in town."

"Oh, I forgot about those!" Happily, Emma slipped off her seat. "We'll see you later, Uncle Jed."

Jamie fell asleep as soon as his head hit the pillow, and after drawing the curtains, Sarah led Emma through to the other bedroom.

"Did you see that flood?" Emma asked as she sat up cross-legged on her mother's bed, her comics spread over her lap. "It was something else!"

Something else, Sarah reflected dismally, didn't even begin to describe it...or the situation resulting from the washed-out track. They were stranded at Morgan's Hope. The timing couldn't have been worse.

Trepidation rippled through her as she anticipated her upcoming encounter with Jed. She'd sensed the tension in him when they met up in the parking lot and it had been easy for her to figure out its cause: he'd learned about Chance's criminal carelessness.

Oh, he'd been pleasant enough on the drive home—and also over lunch—but that would have been because of the children. As soon as he got her on her own, there'd be no holds barred. He'd let his anger loose, and from that moment on till she could finally leave his home, he'd treat her the way he'd treated her in the beginning—with bitterness and hostility.

"Mom, aren't you going downstairs?"

"Yes, Emma. I'm going now."

But it was with reluctant steps that she left the bedroom.

On reaching the landing, she felt her heart lurch when she saw Jed in the foyer. He was lost in scrutiny of one of the oil paintings and didn't hear her tread on the carpet as she walked downstairs.

She swallowed hard when she saw him run a fingertip slowly over the scrawled signature. He must know now that Jeralyn had done these oils. Just as he must know everything else....

She paused at the foot of the stairs and, clutching the newel post, cleared her throat nervously.

He turned. "Ah, there you are. Guess what I found out today. These—" his wide gesture encompassed all three paintings "—were done by my wife."

Where was the animosity she'd expected? Thrown off balance by his casual tone, Sarah could only stare blankly at him.

He obviously misinterpreted her silence because he went on, "Yeah, I was surprised, too! We were wrong in thinking the signature was mine. Take a closer look. You'll see it's *Jer* Morgan, not Jed."

Sarah forced herself to walk over and stand beside him.

"You're right." But even as she spoke, she was asking herself bewilderedly, what was going on? Why was he acting as if nothing was amiss? Was he playing some sort of cat-and-mouse game with her? She stiffened her spine. If she wanted to get the confrontation over with—and she did—it seemed as if she would have to force his hand.

"So—" she fixed him with a steady gaze that belied her jumping nerves "—what else did you find out in town?"

"I found out," he said, "that I had more than

enough money in my bank account to settle things up with Izzio. It's taken care of, Sarah.''

''I can't tell you how grateful I am—''

He cut her off. ''No problem. Are the kids settled in?''

''Yes.''

''We'll talk in the sitting room.''

His tone had become hard and her courage deserted her. ''I...um...need to do the dishes—''

''I've done them.''

Stomach churning, she followed him into the sitting room. He crossed it and flicked on the gas fire, and struggling to control her panic, she walked to the window.

Raindrops ran down the pane, blurring the view. ''How long will it take,'' she asked, ''to get the road repaired?''

''Our track won't be the only one washed out.'' Her throat became dry as she heard him come up behind her. ''And since it serves only three or four houses, it won't be a top priority with the Highways Department.''

''So we could be stranded indefinitely.'' She felt her hair stir against her nape as his breath riffled it. ''Isn't there any other way down the mountain?''

''Not by car. On foot? Sure, but it'd take days to hack through the forest. And that's not something to even remotely consider in this weather—the ground will be a quagmire.''

She was going to explode if he didn't get to the point. If he was now in possession of all the facts regarding Jeralyn's death, he'd assume she'd been aware of Chance's part in it prior to her arrival at

Morgan's Hope. He would believe she had deceived him from the start. Why then wasn't he raging at her? Her tension escalated several notches when he pulled her around to face him.

"Sarah, when I talked to Deborah at the gallery, I learned that I'm a sculptor."

She somehow managed an interested "Mmm!"

"I also learned that I'm a widower." He drew in a deep breath. "Though I think in my heart I already knew it."

There was no point in telling him she'd already found out he'd lost his wife. "It must still have been a shock." Sarah managed to keep her voice steady.

"Yeah, I guess. I didn't get any more out of Deborah because she was in a rush. And I was out of luck when I tried to get Brianna's number."

"Out of luck?"

"Her number's unlisted. I couldn't get to square one with the operator. So in the end I was left with a whole lot of unanswered questions—" He broke off with a frown. "Sarah, you look as if you're going to faint! Are you okay?"

Oh, yes, she did indeed feel faint. Faint with relief. Jed hadn't talked with Brianna. And so he knew none of the details surrounding his wife's death.

A hysterical laugh bubbled up inside her. She barely managed to contain it. "It's just…I just feel so sorry to hear about your loss."

Even as she spoke the words, she felt overwhelmed by guilt. She was being honest in expressing her sympathy for Jed in his loss, but in every other way she was deceiving him…and hating every second of it.

Oh, she still intended telling him the truth about

Chance, but she would wait until she was able to leave. What was the point in telling him now? If she did, the very sight of her would cause him pain…and he'd have to suffer her presence at Morgan's Hope till the road was repaired.

She'd rather live a lie and spare Jed than give him the truth and put him through unnecessary anguish.

She sighed.

"Sarah…"

She blinked as his voice interrupted her despairing thoughts. "Mmm?"

"That was quite a sigh. I sense you have worries you're not sharing. It's no good bottling them up, Sarah. Whatever the problem is, it won't seem so bad if you talk about it. Let me help. If I can."

His kindness almost choked her. How different he'd be if he knew the truth.

"I'm just tired, Jed, after our trip to town." His eyes still probed her, and she flinched inside as she saw the concern there. Oh, how she hated having to deceive him! She felt like a worm. "I think," she said quietly, "that I'll go upstairs and lie down for a while."

"Good idea. And since the rain's tapering off, I'll take Max for a hike. I should have thought of this before, but if my studio's in this general area, Max will surely know where it is. With a bit of luck, he'll lead me to it."

CHAPTER SEVEN

"WHERE have you and Max been, Uncle Jed?"

Jed turned from hanging his navy anorak in the hall closet and saw Emma walking down the stairs. Jamie was behind her, bumping down on his bottom.

"We went for a walk in the woods." As Jed spoke, Max trotted over to the foot of the stairs, wagging his tail as he watched the children descend.

"Mommie's sleeping," Jamie announced, kneeling by Max and giving the dog a warm hug.

"But she'll be wakening soon," Emma added.

Jed said, "I'll make her a cup of tea."

"Can we have a snack, too?" Emma skipped backward ahead of him, swinging Girl in an arc over her head. "Can we have apple juice and one of Mom's chocolate chip cookies?"

"Sure, whatever you want."

By the time the children had finished their snack, the tea was ready. Jed filled two mugs and arranged them on a tray, along with cream and sugar and a teaspoon. Then he added a small plate with a few of the cookies.

"Mom takes just cream, no sugar." Emma lifted Jamie down from his booster seat. "Jamie, wanna play Jenga?"

"Sure!"

The two scurried away, and when Jed walked along to the foyer a minute later, he heard their voices com-

ing from the den. Stepping over Max, he went upstairs.

Sarah's bedroom door was ajar.

He knocked and, getting no answer, pushed the
door open. The curtains were drawn, but in the shadowy light, he could see that her eyes were closed. As
he set the tray on her bedside table, china clinked and
she stirred.

"Hi," he said. "Fancy a cup of tea?"

"Mmm," she responded drowsily. "Yes, please."

He switched on the bedside lamp and she raised
herself on her elbow in a move that tugged down the
neckline of her pink nightie and revealed the swell of
her creamy breasts.

Erotic. Tantalizing.

Forbidden.

He snatched his bedazzled gaze away but too late;
his body had already responded. Mentally, he rolled
his eyes. What kind of a man was he, that he could
lust after a woman who was pregnant? And not only
pregnant, but pregnant with another man's child? Talk
about crass!

But as he poured cream into her tea, the erotic image stubbornly lingered and he saw it again in his
mind's eye—the shadow between the breasts, the twin
puckers on the pink nightie where the peaks caught
on the thin fabric...

He barely managed to suppress a moan.

How many years was it, he wondered grimly, since
he'd made love to a woman? He picked up the teaspoon and stirred her tea. Had he been celibate since
the death of his wife? Even so, his hair-trigger response to a glimpse of feminine flesh was ludicrous.

Surely he was mature enough to have more control of himself?

He was. Of *course* he was!

"There we are." He put down the teaspoon and held out her mug.

She eased herself to a sitting position and tucked her tousled blond hair behind her ears. As she did, he caught a drift of her sweet roses and spicy carnation perfume, along with the heady scent of her skin. A scent that positively exploded with pheromones.

Pheromones that had his name on them....

His hand was unsteady as he gave her the mug.

"Thanks," she murmured. "What a treat."

"Careful," he said. "It's hot."

Not as hot as he was.

He gritted his teeth and, after adding cream and sugar to the other mug, stirred his tea vigorously.

"Where are the children?" she asked.

"Downstairs. Playing with their Jenga." What a mistake he'd made, deciding to have his tea up here in her bedroom. He hadn't anticipated that he'd end up desperately wanting to slide into bed with her. Cupping his hands around his mug, he wandered over to the window. Away from temptation.

"May I have a cookie?"

"Oh...sorry." He recrossed the room, held out the plate and she took one. "What was I thinking?"

He knew only too well what he'd been thinking. He'd been thinking how fantastic it would be to take her breasts in his hands, to cup them, to kiss them—

"Why don't you?" Her voice came to him in a haze. "They're tempting, aren't they?" He blinked and looked at her. She was smiling. "Help yourself," she said. "I can tell by that glint in your eyes that you want to. You'll find them sinfully delicious."

He felt a muscle clench in his groin, felt a wave of desire engulf him. Did fantasies come true? Was she really inviting him to—

"I baked them yesterday." She nibbled on her cookie and squinted up at him. "I know you don't normally eat dessert, but for my chocolate chip cookies you should make an exception. They're out-of-this-world good!"

He'd got their wires crossed. What an utter dolt he was. "Okay, what the heck!" Faking a nonchalant grin, he scooped up a cookie and bit into it. It *was* sinfully delicious. Though not half as delicious as his fantasy.

"You went for your walk?" Sarah asked. "How did it go?"

He gratefully grasped the opportunity to get his mind off sex. "I found my studio."

"You did?" Her eyes brightened. "Where?"

"A few minutes from here—along one of the forest paths. Max headed straight for it when we went out."

She nodded toward the bedside chair. "Sit down and tell me about it."

He slouched down into the chair and stretched his long legs under the bed. "It must have been a cabin at one time, but the main living area has been enlarged and that's the studio part. For the rest, there's a small bedroom, bathroom, kitchen—"

"Do you think that's where you 'camped out'?"

"Oh, without a doubt. Lots of my belongings are over there—clothes, paperwork, books. I guess I must have called the place home for the past six years.'' He took a swig of his tea. ''It would seem that I only recently moved into this house and that I hadn't yet gotten around to moving my stuff over.''

''Did being there bring back any memories?''

''Not a one. There's a sculpture there—of a young woman. The piece was apparently commissioned by the same Greek who commissioned my last work. I found a contract in a filing cabinet.'' He grinned. ''And guess what her name is.''

''Minerva?''

''You're quick. Yup, she's the one. She's to be picked up at the end of the month, as noted on the calendar.''

''I'd like to see her. Will you show me your studio?''

''Sure. We'll take a walk over once you get up.''

Sarah finished her cookie and drank the last of her tea. He finished his own, and as he took her mug, she sank back on her pillows again.

She'd been pale and tired-looking when she went to bed; and now, though her cheeks had some color, he could see that she still looked strained.

When he'd asked what was troubling her, she'd denied anything was wrong. He didn't believe her. Dammit, didn't she trust him? What more could he do to set her mind at rest? He'd already assured her she could stay here as long as she wanted.

Maybe if he tried again, he could coax some answers from her. Maybe if he approached it sideways, she wouldn't notice where he was going with his questions.

''Tell me,'' he said casually, ''about Chance. Apart

from his gambling obsession, what kind of man was my brother?''

Sarah felt a wary prickle at her nape. Talking about Chance presented a challenge: she didn't want to speak ill of him, but at the same time she didn't want to compound her feelings of guilt by adding to her existing deception.

"First of all," Jed went on, "how did you meet?"

That was easy to answer. Sarah felt her tension ease slightly. "I was browsing around a used-car lot in Vancouver with some friends. He was working there—we started talking."

"You said you were...eighteen?"

"Eighteen and immature. I was flattered when he asked me for a date—my friends were gaga about him. He could have had any one of them, but he chose me." She laughed lightly. "I fell for him. He was a charmer—fun, happy-go-lucky. And we seemed to have a lot in common—he told me that other than a brother he wasn't in touch with, he had no family."

"But you did have your mother."

"We lived in the same house, but we might as well have been strangers for all the emotional support she gave me."

"So you found that support in each other." He nodded. "Would I have liked him, Sarah? Sometimes family feuds can arise from some trivial incident, then pride gets in the way of making up."

Sarah was not about to tell him that the reason for this particular feud was far from trivial. "I really don't know." She tried not to sound evasive. "You might have been impatient with him—he was irresponsible in some ways—but he did mean well," she hastened to add, "even though he didn't always keep his promises."

"'The road to hell is paved with good intentions.' Isn't that what they say? But hey, he might have been impatient with me, too. I'm far from perfect myself. So…after the two of you got married, where did you live?"

"He'd been sharing a condo with three buddies, but we figured Vancouver would be too expensive for us when the baby came, so we moved up to Quesnel and rented an apartment there. He was a good salesman and got a job right away, but money was tight at first. I found a baby-sitting job, which helped."

"When did he start gambling?"

"Shortly after we married. He'd stopped smoking just before we met, and…" She paused as she recalled what the drugstore cashier had said. *Ciggy in the sofa.* Had Chance given up smoking because of—

"And?"

She blinked. "Sorry. He rationalized his gambling expenses by saying he just used the money he'd have spent on cigarettes. But it wasn't long before the money he lost at the races far exceeded what he might have spent on smoking."

"When did you decide to call it quits?"

"A few months after Jamie was born. Things had gotten really bad, we fought a lot, and I couldn't live with the stress and uncertainty any longer. I knew it'd be scary going it on my own, but at least I'd be in control."

"Sarah…" Jed hesitated before going on quietly, "Were you still in love with him?"

"I sometimes wonder if what I felt for him in the first place was really love. I believed I was in love with him, but looking back now, I think maybe I was in love with the *idea* of being in love. I'd never had a steady boyfriend before and I was immensely flattered that he wanted me."

"Because he was older, more experienced?"

"Mmm. And he was loaded with charisma. He swept me off my feet—I became pregnant within a week of meeting him. We hadn't taken time to get to know each other. We were lovers but we weren't…friends. I realize now that a man and a woman should become friends before they become lovers. Otherwise, what they have together is just…sex."

"How did you cope financially after you separated?"

"It was hard, but I did manage to make ends meet. I was on my own for a couple of years. Jamie and Emma missed their dad, though, so when he begged me to take him back and swore he'd given up gambling for good, I was foolish enough to believe him. Foolish enough to get pregnant again, too," she added wryly, "though he never knew—he died before I'd found out. Of course," she hastened to add, "I've loved this baby from the moment I learned I was expecting, but—"

"But it was an added burden to an already burdened life." Jed was silent for a few moments before saying, "When did you first find out about Chance's debts?"

"About three months after his death. It had taken Izzio that long to track me down because I'd moved from our apartment to the home of the friend who'd given me the baby-sitting job after Chance died. When Izzio did find me, he put increasing pressure on me to pay back the money he was owed. I gave him what little I could spare from my weekly paycheck, but when I lost my job last week and said I couldn't give him any more money, he became nasty. I felt frightened, cornered. So I—''

"So you came here. Sarah, I wish to hell you'd decided to do that sooner. But at least you're at Morgan's Hope now, Izzio's paid off, and you can put the past behind you.''

"I don't know how I'll ever be able to thank you.''

"Just stay in my life,'' he said, giving her a warm smile. "You and the kids. That's all the thanks I want.'' He lifted the tray. "You get up now and get dressed. When you come down, we'll all take a walk to the studio.''

The afternoon was cool, but the air was fresh and the woods were alive with birdsong.

Sarah, Jed and the children crossed the forecourt to the forest, following Max, who led them eagerly onto the path. It was muddy and rutted, and they walked carefully. After a few minutes, they emerged into a grassy clearing.

"Look!'' Emma shouted. "There it is!''

Sarah looked with interest at the log cabin situated in the middle of the clearing. It had large windows and a shingled roof. Gray wisps drifted from the stubby chimney and she smelled wood smoke.

"You set a fire going?'' she asked Jed as they approached the cabin.

"Woodstove. I lit it earlier to warm the place up. The rooms felt damp."

Once inside, they took off their jackets and then Jed ushered them through to a bright, rectangular room.

"This is it," he said, leaning his hip against a workbench. "My studio."

"Look at that bare-naked lady!" Emma gawked at the sculpture dominating the area. "Uncle Jed, is she for real?"

Sarah crossed to the woodstove and stood with her back to it. The warmth crept over her legs, over her back. It felt good.

"She's as real as the elephant you made with your Play-Doh," Jed said.

"You made her?" Awe tinged Emma's voice.

"That's right, honeybunch."

"If you were in my class at school, you would most definitely get an A," Emma announced firmly. "You have a real knack for modeling, Uncle Jed!"

Sarah smiled as Emma parroted the words Jed had used when he'd admired Emma's elephant. She saw the twinkle in Jed's eyes and knew he was as amused as she was.

"Yeah," he said, straight-faced, "so I've been told."

Jamie had found a pile of small rocks under the window. Sliding down on his knees, he started playing with them.

"Can I help you, Jamie?" Without waiting for an answer, Emma sat down beside him. "Let's build a tower."

Jed had moved over to the sculpture and, with a

look of concentration, was running a hand slowly over the alabaster-white shoulders. Sarah sensed he was immersed in his thoughts, trying to dredge up memories.

What beautiful hands he has, she reflected, letting her gaze linger on them. An artist's hands, elegant and sensitive, yet strong and practical. The fingers were long, the smattering of hair on the back crisp and black....

How would it feel to have those fingers on her? As the thought sneaked up on her, she felt a shiver of excitement. Unlike the cold, hard surface of the marble figure, her skin was warm and smooth; her flesh firm yet resilient—

"Sarah?"

She jerked her gaze from his hands. Jed was looking at her with a questioning expression in his eyes.

"Oh, sorry." She hoped he'd think the heat from the stove had caused the sudden flush in her cheeks. "My mind drifted for a moment. So...how about showing me the rest of the cabin?"

"Sure." He shrugged. "Though there's not much else to see. It's all pretty poky."

It was. The bathroom was tiny, the kitchen only slightly bigger. The bedroom was about twelve feet square and furnished in a spartan manner with a single bed, maple dresser and matching bedside table.

"It appears I used this as a storage area," Jed said as they stood just inside the doorway. "As well as for sleeping. There's hardly room left to swing a mouse."

Sarah's attention was caught by a framed photo on

the bedside table. She could see it was a wedding photo of a formally attired couple.

She gestured toward it. ''Is that you and your wife?''

''Must be. Looking at it didn't bring back any memories, though. Frustrating as hell.''

''May I have a look?''

''Sure.''

Jed reached over a large cardboard box to get the pewter-framed photo. As he handed it to Sarah, his thumb brushed her wrist and a current of electricity crackled through her.

Her pulse gave a jolt. This kind of thing had never happened to her with anyone else...not even with Chance. Her physical awareness of her brother-in-law was sexual and raw...and unwelcome. Not to mention inappropriate! Even if she were foolish enough to fall in love with him, this man was forbidden to her. Because of the past.

She tried to focus on the photo, but as her eyes fixed determinedly on the couple—Jed movie star good-looking in a black tux, Jeralyn stunningly beautiful in a white lace gown—all she could think of was the man at her shoulder, his breath disturbing her hair, his earthy scent disturbing her senses. Destroying her equilibrium.

''How did you feel when you looked at this picture?'' Sarah deplored the sexy huskiness of her voice. ''Didn't you remember *anything?*''

''No. But I did get a...feeling when I looked at Jeralyn.''

She turned her head to him. ''What kind of a feeling?''

"Sadness. A kind of…ache, deep inside me."

His eyes reflected that sadness now. Sarah felt her heart go out to him. "Your memory *will* come back." But not, she prayed, till after she and the children were many miles from Morgan's Hope. "And it probably won't be when you're trying desperately to dig it out. It's more likely to hit you when you're least expecting it."

She moved away from him and, reaching over the cardboard box, set the picture on the table. As she straightened, she felt a dull throb start up at the base of her spine.

With a sigh, she rubbed a hand over it.

"What's wrong?" Jed asked.

"Oh, nothing much…just a bit of an ache."

"Would a massage help?"

"Oh, I don't need—"

"Sit on the edge of the bed." His tone brooked no argument.

She sat.

He sat beside her and turned her so she was facing away from him. "Relax," he said, and she felt him sweep aside her long hair to let it fall forward over her left breast.

Then his fingers took possession of her shoulders, kneading, caressing, expertly probing. She gave herself up to the sensation. It was irresistible; the sheer luxury of skillful hands soothing away all the knots, the tightness.

She closed her eyes. "If you ever decide to give up sculpting," she murmured as he worked his way down, "you could make a fortune massaging the rich and famous."

He chuckled and started massaging the small of her back. "That could be fun. More fun than working with marble—" He broke off as she winced. "A tender spot?"

"Yes, but keep digging there. It hurts but it feels good, if that makes any sense!"

He worked on her for a full five minutes, and by that time, she felt so relaxed she was almost asleep.

"That's it," he murmured. "Feel better?"

"Much." She raised her arms and flipped her hair back over her shoulders. "Thanks, that was great."

Turning, she smiled at him.

A smile that dazzled Jed. Just as her glossy blond hair dazzled him, and her beautiful gray eyes dazzled him. Her cheeks were as flushed as they'd been as she stood by the woodstove; a flush that made her glow.

A flush that deepened as their eyes locked.

"Sarah…"

He reached out to capture a strand of hair that had slipped from behind her ear. It sifted through his fingers like the finest silk. He leaned closer as he tucked the strand into place, and his fingertips brushed her earlobe.

She shuddered.

And the air crackled between them. Just as he'd felt it crackle when he'd handed her the photo earlier and had accidentally brushed her wrist. He'd managed to ignore the electricity then, had managed to ignore his body's instantaneous response. But now, sitting on the bed with her, the raw sexual attraction thrumming between them was impossible to ignore. Impossible to deny.

He slid his hand down her arm to her wrist. He wove his fingers through hers. Palm to palm.

She drew in a shaky breath. Their eyes remained locked. Hers were cloudy, unfocused; his own felt heavy.

His heartbeats slowed to a hammering thud.

Her lips parted on a tiny moan. Moist lips; full, pink, expectant.

''I'm going to kiss you,'' he whispered.

''I know—''

His mouth was on hers, taking in her answer. Her kiss was open and hot, her hair a tumble around his fingers as he clasped her head with his hands. As their kiss deepened, it became more intimate by the second.

He wanted her. And she wanted him.

Her arms were around his neck, dragging him urgently closer. As he slid his mouth along her jaw, against the scented sensitive spot below her ear, she let her head fall back, and he heard her sigh of surrender.

Her fingertips dug into his nape, the nails like dull claws raking his skin. He buried his face against her skin, drank in the musky female scent of her. His hands were on her breasts and he felt them become swollen and rigid.

She dragged his face back to hers, sought his lips again desperately. He was lost. Lost in lust, and a craving for completion. Blood rushed in his ears, rushed to his groin. He was fast losing control—

''Mommie?'' Jamie's voice came from the door. ''Emma's gone.''

For a frozen second, neither Jed nor Sarah moved.

Then slowly, they drew back from each other and looked at Jamie.

"Gone?" Sarah's voice had a vague quality, as if she were waking from a deep sleep. "What do you mean, Jamie?"

"Gone." He sounded truculent. "With Max."

"They…went out?" Sarah pushed herself up off the bed.

Jed stood, too, and grasped her arm to steady her. He sensed that her desire had been supplanted by anxiety. His own desire had cooled. Somewhat. And temporarily.

"Max needed to go." Jamie scowled. "Emma told me stay here."

"She's probably on the doorstep," Sarah said. "Waiting for him to come back."

Jed nodded. "Sure." He glanced at his watch. "It's time we were getting over to the house anyway. I need to get dinner started."

But Emma wasn't outside on the doorstep. Nor was there any sign of her or the dog in the clearing.

Frowning, Sarah glanced back into the entryway. "Her jacket's gone."

"When she let Max out," Jed said, "he may have made for the house and she'll have gone after him. Let's check."

She wasn't in the house. And she wasn't anywhere in the gardens. When they finished their search, they ended up back at the front door. Jed had been carrying Jamie on his shoulders; now he swung the little boy down onto the stoop.

"Where can she be?" Distraughtly, Sarah looked

up at Jed. "Could she have followed Max into the forest?"

Jed's expression was grim. "It's possible."

Sarah's stomach gave an unpleasant heave.

"Sarah, take Jamie and go inside. I'll look for them."

"I want to come, too!"

"You'll only be a hindrance." His tone was gentle. "I'll cover more ground on my own."

Sarah bit her lip on a protest. "You're right," she said. "But it's not going to be easy, just waiting."

He put his arms around her and gave her a reassuring hug. "We'll be back before you know it."

But darkness had fallen before Jed returned. Jamie was in bed; and Sarah had spent the intervening time alternately pacing the sitting room and standing at the window, her frantic gaze searching the near-black night, her heart ripped apart with worry.

Suddenly, the sensors clicked on the light above the front door and she saw Jed. His powerful legs were taking him with urgent strides toward the house.

And he was carrying Emma in his arms.

CHAPTER EIGHT

JED had noticed Sarah at the window as he approached the front door, and walking into the house he saw her hurry from the sitting room.

When she saw him, she swayed a little and he thought she was going to pass out. No wonder, he reflected, after what she must have gone through while she was waiting. But he had to admire the way she gathered herself together, straightening her shoulders before walking quickly across to him.

"Is she all right?" Her gaze had zeroed in on Emma, and when she saw that the child's eyes were closed, the small face white beneath grubby tear smudges, she inhaled a sharp breath.

"Relax, Sarah." Jed stood aside to let Max limp past him into the foyer. "She's fine, doesn't have hypothermia, didn't get that cold."

"Oh, thank heaven!"

"She's just tired and sleepy." Jed shoved the door shut with his hip.

"Where did you find her?"

Emma's eyes flickered open. "I fell into a gully and Max climbed down to help me." Her voice shook. "But then he slipped and rolled under a big log and got trapped and he couldn't get out and he's hurt his leg." The words caught on a sob. "And it's all my fault."

"Hush. He's going to be fine. You both are." She

119

gave Emma a tight hug. "It's cold out. It's lucky that you were wearing your quilted jacket—"

"And lucky that the spot where she fell was dry," Jed added. "But she could do with a warm-up. Could you fetch a blanket from upstairs?"

"Sure." Sarah lovingly smoothed back Emma's disheveled hair before making for the stairs.

Jed carried Emma into the sitting room, where the leaping gas flames were a welcome sight. Max—poor Max—limped over to the hearth and, after circling awkwardly a couple of times, lay down and began licking his sore leg.

It wasn't broken, just grazed—Jed had quickly checked it when he'd rescued him from under the log. He'd give it a more thorough check later. Emma was his first priority.

He lowered himself into an armchair by the fire and felt his heart soften as he looked at the child's face.

How dear she had become to him, he realized. And again he felt the indescribable relief and euphoria that had swept over him when he found her. He'd known her only a few days, but already he felt as close to Emma as if she were his own.

Sarah paused in the doorway, emotion bringing a lump to her throat when she saw how tenderly Jed was looking at Emma.

He loved the child; there was no doubt about it. And Emma adored him right back. But heartbreak lay in wait for both of them. And it lay in wait for her, too.

When Jed had walked in the front door, bringing Emma home, he'd seemed to Sarah the very epitome of what a hero should be. Something had melted inside her. He was tall, dark and handsome, of course, but she was way past being dazzled by mere good looks—Chance had cured her of that! What she found in Jed was something so much more. Something that drew her in a way she'd never experienced before.

And she'd realized, at that moment, with a shock that made her giddy, that she had unexpectedly, unbelievably and unconditionally, fallen in love with him.

And oh, what a fool she had been to let that happen.

"Sarah?"

Swallowing hard, she swiftly refocused her thoughts and, walking over to Jed, gave him the heavy wool blanket.

After he'd wrapped it cosily around Emma, Sarah sat on an ottoman and, pulling Emma onto her knee, held her close while Jed examined Max's leg, his touch gentling when the dog winced.

"Uncle Jed," Emma said worriedly, "is he going to need a splint?"

"No, the leg's not broken." Jed straightened. "He'll be fine. So…what happened, Emma? How come the two of you ended up where you did?"

"Max went chasing after a rabbit when I let him out to do his business. It was a cute little bunny and I wanted to see where he went, too, so I grabbed my jacket and ran after them."

"And did you find out where the bunny lived?" Jed asked in a teasing tone.

"No, but I did try. Even harder than Max. I just kept going on and on into the forest after Max wanted to turn back. He kept barking at me to follow him home, but I wouldn't. So finally he gave in and came with me.''

"That's because he wanted to look after you," Jed said.

"After he got his leg stuck, I snuggled up to him so he'd keep me from getting too cold," Emma said. "And he did. He's my favorite pet in all the world and I'm going to love him forever.''

"Sounds like a plan to me!" Jed smiled. "Now, how about something to eat?"

"No thanks, Uncle Jed. I'm not hungry."

Sarah frowned. "You have to have something, Emma. How about some soup and a sandwich?"

"How about a mug of hot chocolate?" Emma countered.

"I'll get it." Jed rose from his chair.

"After you have your drink," Sarah said to Emma, "I'm going to pop you in a bath and then—"

"Mom!" Emma's expression was aghast. "I've lost Girl!"

"When did you last have her?"

"I don't know!" Emma wailed. "I can't remember!"

"She's at the studio," Jed said. "I remember seeing her on my way out. She was sitting on my statue's big toe!"

Emma gave a shaky giggle. "Yes, I remember now. Uncle Jed, can you get her for me?"

"Emma, can't it wait till morning?" But even as she asked the question, Sarah knew what the answer would be. Emma could not, would not, spend one night without Girl.

"No, Mom, you *know* I need her. Will you, Uncle Jed? Pretty please with a cherry on the top?"

He chuckled and made for the door. "I'll go over there just as soon as I've brought your hot chocolate."

"And after you drink that," her mother said firmly, "it's a quick bath and then off to bed for you, young lady. You've had a very tiring day."

"Tired, Sarah?" Jed leaned back in his kitchen chair and looked across the table at Sarah, who had just finished her makeshift dinner and was folding her serviette.

"I am," she said. "A bit." She pushed back her chair and got to her feet. "I'll just tidy up in here, then I'm off to bed. But first, I want to thank you again for finding Emma. I was worried sick. I kept thinking about that runaway creek and—"

"Yeah, I know." Jed got up. "I was feeling pretty sick myself. Anyway, they're both home safe now, so you can quit worrying and—"

Sarah gasped. And pressed her hands to the small of her back.

Jed took a step toward her. "What's wrong?"

She gave a rueful smile. "It was just a sudden stab of pain. I guess the baby must have pressed on a nerve."

"You don't think you're in...you know?"

She laughed. "Labor?"

"What's so funny?" He sounded petulant.

"Your face. If you could only see it!"

He heard a distinctly accusatory note in his voice as he retorted, "It doesn't cause you any concern that you could have your baby…here? With no doctor, no nurses?''

"It's not going to happen. I told you before. I'm always late. And I had a couple of false alarms with both Emma and Jamie. Believe me, when the real thing starts, I'll recognize it. Trust me, I'm experienced.''

"You may be experienced, but you're just so damned young!"

"I'm not so young, Jed." Her eyes twinkled. "Maybe it just seems that way to you because you're so ancient!"

"Ancient?" He drew down his brow in a scowl. "Thirty-four's *ancient*?"

"Oh, definitely. It's different for a woman, of course. She's just reaching her prime at thirty-five, whereas a man's past it by that time. The male of the species peaks around the age of eighteen and it's downhill from there on in!" She sounded as if she could hardly contain her laughter.

"You're talking *sexual* peak?"

Sarah saw the sly challenge in his eyes and knew she'd walked right into it. Uh-oh! But better to barge on than back down. "Yes." She cleared her throat. "*Sexual* peak."

"So what you're suggesting—" his eyes were narrowed "—is that a man my age couldn't…keep up…with a younger woman. In the, um, bedroom."

"I'm not *suggesting* it." Sarah gave him her most wide-eyed gaze. "I'm giving you the statistics."

"Statistics be damned!" With an exaggeratedly sexy leer, he said, "If you weren't in the family way,

I'd prove to you that there are exceptions to every rule!''

Sarah barely managed to suppress a chuckle. "How disappointing...for both of us, that we can't put you to the test.''

"As you say, disappointing. But then, I'm not a man who takes disappointment lightly. My problem is—'' he started walking toward her ''—that I can't recall how I felt at eighteen. But I can tell you how I feel right now.''

Sarah tried to draw back, but she was up against the counter. "And how is that?'' She sounded breathless. "How do you feel right now?''

"Lady,'' he drawled, "I'm in my prime!'' He clasped her shoulders and looked directly into a pair of startled gray eyes. "Maybe we can do some...*preliminary* testing!''

Her lips parted in a protest that he demolished with a demanding kiss. He let her up for air and she gasped, "The statistics say—''

"To hell with the statistics,'' he growled. "This isn't about statistics!'' And he kissed her again.

For six heartbeats, she didn't respond; on the seventh, she put her arms around his neck and kissed him back with a passion that sent blood racing to his groin. He slid his arms around her and pulled her close. He felt the hard bulge of her belly, but the knowledge that she was pregnant with his brother's child no longer bothered him. No longer made him feel he ought to keep his distance. He thought of the baby now as just Sarah's; and he thought of it with the same affection he thought of Emma and Jamie.

Family. They were family. The knowledge made

him dizzy—dizzy with longing to make Sarah his own.

He groaned and deepened his kiss. It was like sinking into heaven. Sweet, ineffably sweet. He slid his hands under her shirt, followed her bra to the front, glided his fingertips up till they reached the tip of her breasts.

He felt her stiffen, then her lips slackened, her body yielded. He thought he heard her whisper, "Yes..."

But even as he did, he felt something small and hard poke his stomach. And poke it again. It was a fist, punching. Or it was a bent knee, gouging. Or it was a tiny foot, kicking.

He smiled and, with his mouth still close to Sarah's, said, "Did you feel that?"

"Feel what?" Her eyes opened and she looked foggily up at him.

He took his hands from under her shirt and looped his arms around her back. "The baby," he said with a chuckle. "He doesn't approve of what we're doing. He kicked me."

Her eyes gradually focused, and he saw the glimmer of laughter in them. Mocking laughter. "Thank heavens somebody in the family knows where to draw the line!"

Her tone was flippant but her cheeks were flushed. The lady wasn't as blasé, Jed guessed, as she tried to appear.

"But the little guy won't be in there forever," he said with a mischievous grin. "And after that, it'll be no holds barred."

He might as well have tossed a grenade in the air; he could feel tension snap into place between them.

"Jed, I won't even be here then." Her voice was quiet. "You know I'm leaving as soon as the track's repaired."

"Yeah," he said. "I know you can't wait to get back to civilization. But I'm going to miss you. You *and* the kids. It's going to be lonely at Morgan's Hope after you're all gone." He withdrew from her and crossed to the window, where he stood staring out into the dark. "Lonely as hell."

Sarah stood at her bedroom window, looking out into the dark. Wistfully, she remembered how she'd felt when Jed had kissed her. All her worries had floated away and she had lost herself in the bliss of having his arms around her. She was so in love with him, she could barely stand it.

And he had no idea she felt that way about him.

Oh, he must know she found him sexually appealing—the passionate way she'd returned his kiss would have told him that. What he didn't know was that she longed desperately to stay on at Morgan's Hope. With him.

But it was not to be.

Any day now, the track would be repaired. And the moment it happened, she'd have to pack Emma and Jamie and all their belongings into the Cutlass and drive away.

Away from this little corner of heaven.

She opened the window and inhaled a deep breath of the clean night air. From the highway she heard the rumble of traffic; and from the forest she heard the hoot of an owl, the lonesome sound finding an echo in her own desolation.

From now on, she decided with a bleak sigh, she'd keep her distance from Jed—both physically and emotionally. She had to cool down his interest in her because the more he grew to like her, the greater his feelings of betrayal would be when he learned of her deceit.

It might hurt him a little now to be treated with indifference; but it would save him from a greater hurt in the future. The end, Sarah decided, would surely, in this case, justify the means.

Jed stood in the open doorway of his study watching Sarah.

Three days had passed since their kiss in the kitchen, and during those three days she'd treated him like a piece of furniture. No, actually she treated the furniture better. Take right how. She was vigorously polishing his mahogany desk as if her sole aim in life was to buff it to brilliance.

"Sarah…"

She turned with a gasp. "Jed. I didn't hear you come in. Did you and the children enjoy your walk?"

She was wearing a soft blue shirt over a pair of taupe jeans, and her blond hair shimmered in the sunshine streaming in through the window. She looked so beautiful he wanted to sweep her into his arms and…

And he knew that what he wanted was totally inappropriate, considering her condition. Not to mention X-rated. Maybe, in some countries, even illegal.

He said, "Don't you think you're overdoing it?"

"I feel fine." She flicked her yellow cloth and dust

motes drifted into the sun's rays. "Bursting with energy."

"Then why didn't you come with us?" he drawled. "When I suggested we all go out, you said you felt a bit tired."

She flushed. "I just, er…" Her stumbling response faded to silence.

"Wanted to be alone." His tone had an edge of irony. "Or rather, wanted not to be with me. Am I right?"

She met his gaze steadily. "No, of course not."

"It was the kiss, wasn't it?"

She looked as if she wanted to run, but she held her ground. After a long pause, she said, "It was…a mistake." Her voice was so low he could barely hear her. "A mistake I don't want to repeat."

"Wouldn't it have been more honest to have just said that in the beginning?"

"Maybe more honest." She lowered her gaze to the duster in her hands. "But…more difficult."

"Yeah. I guess it can't be easy for a woman to tell a man she finds his kisses repulsive."

She snapped her head up, her eyes wide with dismay. "Oh, but I didn't find—" She clamped her lips shut. And if her face had been flushed before, it was now red as an overripe strawberry.

"Hah." Jed couldn't suppress a chuckle. "Gotcha!" He closed the space between them and, taking the duster from her fingers, tossed it aside. "Okay, now that we've settled that you don't find me repulsive—" he tipped her chin as she would have turned away and made her look at him "—then what's the harm in a few kisses?"

She cleared her throat. "Kisses can lead to…other things."

"Sarah, I'm not an animal. For Pete's sake, you're eight months pregnant."

"I wasn't thinking of…that." Her sigh seemed to come from the depths of her soul. "I was thinking of…emotional involvement."

He'd never seen lashes so luxuriant, so long. They skimmed her cheeks as her eyelids flickered. Her skin was perfect, too. Smooth, silky smooth, and just begging to be touched. He thrust his fingers into the hip pockets of his jeans to keep them under control. For the moment. "We're talking now," he said softly, "about falling in love."

"I didn't say anything about…about…*that*!" She sounded as if she was finding it hard to grab gulps of air into her lungs. "I just said—"

"Sarah, let's admit it. We're attracted to each other. And we like each other. Falling in love is a distinct possibility…so why fight it? And if it doesn't happen, we'll settle for friendship."

"It's not that simple."

"Because you're still in love with my brother?"

"I've already told you I'm not."

"Then what?"

She twisted her wedding ring. Jed was sure she didn't even know she was doing it. "Somebody," she said, "could get hurt."

"I'm willing to take that chance. Are you?"

She ignored his question. "You don't know anything about me. What if…when your memory comes back…there'll be something…" She swallowed hard and then went on in a rush as if she wanted to get the words over and done with. "...something you don't remember, something in your past, that would make you not want me around?"

He took her hands in his, stopped her twirling her gold ring. "Sarah, we've become friends, right? We get along well...when you're not treating me like a leper."

"Sorry." She grimaced. "Yes, we do get along well."

"Then let's continue to be friends and see where it leads. I promise that from now on I won't try to kiss you. But—" his eyes twinkled "—if you should ever feel a pressing need to kiss me, I'll do nothing to stop you. In fact, I'll do my best to cooperate. Is it a deal?"

She chewed her lip, withdrew into her thoughts. Troubled thoughts, if he was any judge. But in the end, she nodded.

"Okay." She smiled, but he sensed the smile was forced. "You've got yourself a deal."

But please don't blame me if you're the one who gets hurt.

Sarah hadn't said the words aloud, but she'd said them in her head. And at the same time, she'd been appalled that she was agreeing to his open-ended plan. Yet what other option had she had? How could she not agree to be friends?

Besides, she decided as she moved around the kitchen preparing dinner, it was working out well so far. She and Jed had played cards in the den while the children had napped after lunch, and they'd had fun. Then they'd taken Max and Emma and Jamie for a walk down the track, and that had been fun, too. Jed had held her hand in case she slipped on the sometimes muddy road, but his clasp had been casual, not intimate. Yes, everything had gone well....

Until they'd reached the place where the track had been destroyed by the creek and found a couple of workmen on the other side, assessing the situation.

"We're starting on this tomorrow," one of them called across to Jed in answer to Jed's shouted query. "First thing. Should be finished by Friday."

Sarah's heart had plummeted. Another three days and she'd be driving down here for the last time.

"Three more days." Jed tightened his grip on her hand as they started back up the track. "I thought— hoped—we'd have longer."

"But you knew I'd be leaving—"

"Yeah. But it would have been much more convenient if you'd been staying on here."

"Convenient for what?"

"For getting to know each other better," he said.

It wasn't going to happen, she could have told him. But didn't.

"Before you leave," he said, "I'm going to give you money—"

"No, Jed. Thank you, but you've already loaned me enough—"

"That was to pay off Chance's debts."

"He was my husband. His debts were mine. And I will pay you back one day. But I wouldn't even consider taking more money from you for my own use."

"It's not only for you, dammit, it's for the kids— for your family, Sarah!"

"Try to understand," she said wearily. "I don't like being beholden. It's just something I...can't. Nothing you can say will persuade me to take any more of your money." His brows had tugged down in a dark scowl. She said, "Don't worry, Jed. I'm one of those people who always land on their feet." She moved quickly to change the subject. "Now let's get back to the house. The afternoon's cooling off and I'm ready for a nice hot cup of tea."

She could sense he wanted to continue the pressure, but he must also have sensed her resolution, so he backed off.

When they reached the house, he set a hand on her arm. "You put the kettle on. I'm going over to the studio. When I popped by there this morning, I came upon a cardboard box full of paperwork—letters, receipts and suchlike. Probably all the mail that arrived when I was living at the cabin. I'm going to bring the box over here and go through it tonight. Who knows what I might find out? You can help if you like— many hands make light work, right?"

Without waiting for a response, he took off across the forecourt.

Sarah stared after him, her eyes wide with dismay. What would happen if one of those letters contained the information she'd been so desperately hiding from Jed?

CHAPTER NINE

"WELL, that explains it."

Sarah raised her gaze from the receipt she'd been scanning and looked at Jed. They'd divided the contents of the cardboard box into two piles. She was sitting behind the desk with one; he was sitting at the other side of the desk with the second. "Explains what?" she asked.

"I've wondered how I ended up in possession of those paintings in the front hall." He waved a letter at her. "This is from Deborah Feigelman. She sends condolences on my wife's death, then goes on to say she still has three of Jer's oils in her gallery and did I want her to sell them as per her contract with Jer or send them back to Morgan's Hope."

"You must have been thrilled to get them. Any of your wife's paintings that had been in your home at the time of the fire would probably have been ruined."

"Yeah, I..." Jed's brows gathered in a frown. "How did you know...about the fire?"

Sarah wished the floor would open and swallow her up. "Didn't...you...tell me?" She stumbled over the words, knowing full well that Jed had never mentioned the fire.

He continued to gaze at her.

"No?" She shifted awkwardly in her seat. "Oh, I remember now. The cashier at the drugstore—the day we were in town—*she* was the one who told me. She noticed me looking at a framed print of one of your wife's paintings—it was hanging in the store…and she…''

Jed tossed the letter onto the desk. ''Since I never brought the matter up, did you assume I didn't know?''

''No,'' Sarah said. ''I assumed you *did* know.''

Silence stretched uncomfortably between them.

He was the one who eventually broke it. ''What else did you find out that day?''

Sarah slid a hand into the folds of her shirt and surreptitiously crossed her fingers. ''Nothing.''

''Nothing?''

''The woman wanted to gossip.'' Sarah managed to meet his gaze steadily. ''I didn't.''

''Even though you knew I was anxious to find out everything I could about—''

''I knew you were anxious, yes, but I didn't want to find out that way. It seemed…sleazy.'' Sarah's chin lifted. ''When we met up again, you seemed distraught, so I assumed you'd already discovered what happened. And then when you didn't bring it up, I decided you didn't want to talk about it. I assumed you found it too…upsetting.''

''The reason I didn't talk about it was that I didn't want to upset *you*.''

His consideration for her made her own deception even more intolerable. ''Who told *you* about it?'' she asked.

''The caretaker at the town cemetery. And I gathered from him,'' he added with a self-derisive smile, ''that I'd become a hermit.''

"That may have been true in the past," Sarah said, "but you've been very hospitable to us."

"Maybe I've changed."

"Yes," she said quietly. "Maybe you have."

"Or maybe it's because you're family." After a moment, he went on, "Sarah, for whatever reason, we both kept quiet about the fire, but from now on let's keep the lines of communication open and not risk any more misunderstandings. Let's be totally honest with each other, okay?"

Avoiding his direct gaze, Sarah picked up the next envelope in her pile. With a sense of alarm, she saw that the return address was Brianna's.

"Sarah?"

Jerking her gaze up, she found to her relief that his attention was fixed on her, not on what was in her hand.

"All right," she said. "Let's do that." Keeping her eyes locked with his, she slid the envelope under her pile of papers. "Now if you don't mind, I'm going to call it a night." Planting her hands on the desk for support, she rose from her chair. "We've been at this for a couple of hours and I'm feeling a bit tired."

Jed got up, too, and stretched. "Yeah," he said, "it's getting late. We'll finish the job tomorrow. You go on upstairs now and I'll make some hot chocolate, bring it to your room."

They walked out to the foyer together. When they reached the foot of the stairs, Jed patted her shoulder and said, "Up you go."

Sarah suppressed her frustration. She'd hoped Jed would head straight on to the kitchen, giving her the chance to slip back and grab Brianna's letter. Instead, he stood there, a hand on the newel post, waiting for her to ascend.

She had no option but to do so. And he stayed at the foot of the stairs till she reached the landing before he finally took off along the corridor to the kitchen.

She could have gone back down then, but she was afraid to risk it. What if he heard her and came back only to find her sneaking into the study? What excuse could she possibly give that would satisfy him?

No, better if she went to bed now and returned downstairs later after he was asleep. That way, she could read the letter without being disturbed. And if there was anything in it that she didn't want Jed to see, she'd hide it away until the day she left.

Jed tapped on Sarah's bedroom door and, getting no answer, pushed the door open. In the pink glow of the bedside lamp, he could see that she was in bed. And as he set her mug on the bedside table, he saw she was asleep.

He looked down at her and felt an odd twisting in his heart. How beautiful she was. Her blond hair lay like pale silk on the pillow; her lashes made a dusky shadow on her skin. The delicacy of her features made him want to trace a fingertip over her nose, her eyebrows, her cheekbones...

The sweetness of her face made him want to kiss her.

Taking in a deep breath, he leaned over and was about to give in to the temptation when he suddenly remembered the promise he'd made—the promise not to kiss her again...with the proviso that if she ever felt a pressing need to kiss him, she must, of course, act on it.

He smiled, a self-mocking smile, and just looked at her for another long moment instead, letting her image imprint itself indelibly on his mind before he left the room.

The raucous shriek of a crow woke Sarah with a start.

What a deep sleep she'd been in. A deep and dreamless sleep. She stirred and stretched. And then, heaving her body up to a sitting position, she leaned back against the headboard and drowsily brushed her hair from her eyes.

Dawn was breaking.

Light filtered into the room, revealing the mug of hot chocolate on her bedside table—only it was no longer hot.

She realized she must have fallen asleep the moment she slid between the sheets. And panic shattered her early-morning lethargy as she remembered her plan to sneak down and read Brianna's letter. That plan had come to naught.

Distractedly, she ran a soothing hand over her bulge as the baby changed position. She had to go down *now* and read the letter, check its contents, hide it if necessary.

Pushing aside the covers in a swift movement, she got up. After a hurried trip to the bathroom, she put on slippers and housecoat and crept out to the corridor.

A board creaked under her foot as she passed Jed's room. She froze, listened for a long moment for any sound behind his door. She heard nothing. She continued on her way, her nerves jumping with every step she took.

She didn't relax till she had the envelope safely in her hand. Then she sank onto the swivel chair behind the desk and eased out Brianna's letter. Spreading the flimsy paper out on the desktop, she started to read.

"So...did you catch the worm?"

Sarah thought her heart would stop when she heard Jed's voice. Resisting the automatic urge to cover the letter with the flat of her hands, she looked up and saw him in the doorway. "What do you mean?"

Tucking his black T-shirt into the waist of his jeans, he said teasingly, "The early bird?"

"Oh." Somehow she managed a smile. "No, I wasn't looking to catch any worms. I just woke early and knew I wouldn't get back to sleep, so I decided to come downstairs."

"Yeah, I heard you go past my door. I threw my clothes on and got up, thinking it might have been Emma or—"

His words were drowned out as Max gave a demanding yelp from the foyer.

He turned away. "Gotta go and let him out." He added over his shoulder, "I'll be right back. Then we can have breakfast together—maybe we'll have half an hour of peace and quiet before the kids come down!"

As she watched him leave, Sarah blew out a sigh of relief. What a narrow escape. What if he'd asked to see the letter?

She'd finished reading it just before he appeared and it had confirmed her worst fears. Brianna had written it shortly after Jeralyn's death, and in it she bemoaned Chance's carelessness and the fact that his smoking had caused the fatal fire. Brianna ended by saying she understood why Jed never wanted to set eyes on Chance again. She, too, wanted to forget his brother had ever existed.

As Sarah heard the front door slam shut, she hurriedly folded the letter, stuffed it back into the envelope and plunged it deep into the slash pocket of her housecoat.

''You were asleep last night,'' Jed said as he slotted his breakfast dishes into the dishwasher, ''when I brought up your hot chocolate.''

''I overdid things yesterday.'' Leaning forward in her chair, Sarah ran a vitamin pill from the bottle onto her palm. ''I went out like a light as soon as I got into bed.''

''How do you feel today?''

''Okay. Maybe a bit draggy.'' She tipped back her head and swallowed the pill with a gulp of milk from her glass.

Jed compressed his lips grimly as he scrutinized her. She looked more than ''a bit draggy''. She looked totally washed out. It was intolerable that the road was still impassable; he couldn't even take her to see a doctor.

Sidestepping Max, who was licking up the last morsels of food from his doggy bowl, he moved to the wall phone and jerked the receiver to his ear. No sound. He rattled the plunger. Still nothing. He cursed under his breath.

''No luck?''

He replaced the receiver. "No luck."

As he turned, he tripped over Max, who had fin-ished his breakfast and was walking away from his empty dish. Thrown off balance, Jed lurched forward, cracking his temple against the corner of the island before clattering to the floor on his hands and knees.

Groggily getting back to his feet, he scrubbed the heel of his hand against his temple. "Ouch," he said, "that…"

He blinked. And swayed. He was vaguely aware that Sarah had walked over to him, was grasping his upper arm.

He was also vaguely aware that she was speaking, but his mind had splintered off in different directions. Gold stars sparked in front of his eyes…and images swam in and out of his consciousness. Images of a dark-haired woman with luminous brown eyes and a glorious mass of dancing black curls. She was smiling at him. Holding her arms out to him. Bluebells. She was drifting toward him through a haze of blue-bells.…

"My memory." His voice shook. "It's…starting to come back. I…see…"

Sarah's grip tightened. "See what?"

"Jeralyn. And a house. A rambling old house with a red roof…and…"

"What else, Jed? What else do you see?"

He sensed she was holding her breath just as he was holding his; willing the images to stay, aching to see more. But like ghosts disappearing into a mist, they faded away, leaving him with a sick feeling of disappointment.

"That's all," he muttered hopelessly. "Just Jeralyn, and the house—"

"Mom?" Emma's voice drifted from the foyer.

Sarah looked hesitantly at Jed, then dropping her hand from his arm, called out, "Here, Emma…we're in the kitchen."

"Come on, Jamie, hurry up!" Emma's voice was followed by the patter of running feet.

With a deep sigh, Jed moved over to the window and looked out. How odd it had been, seeing Jeralyn that way…like a stranger, yet someone he had once loved.

"It's a beginning," Sarah said from behind. "Now that you've started to remember, it'll all come back soon."

Which was, of course, what she dreaded.

Hoping to keep Jed away from the waiting paperwork with its potentially explosive contents, she suggested, after breakfast, that they all go for a walk.

"You go ahead." Jed made an absent gesture. "I'd like to finish going through that box of letters."

"Why don't you wait till later? I'll help you."

"No, I want to get on with it."

He seemed detached. It was as if his determination to know more about his past had drawn him into another world, one of which she wasn't a part. And there was nothing she could do about it without arousing his suspicion.

So since it was a fine day, she took the children and Max for a long walk. But all the while the question pounded in her brain: What might Jed find out while she was gone?

When they returned to the house, it was after eleven and trepidation churned through her as she entered the foyer. But when Jed came out of the study, it was obvious from his defeated expression that he'd learned nothing new.

Relief made her feel heady.

"No joy?" she asked.

"Waste of time." He relieved her of her light jacket and hung it in the closet.

"Have you gone through everything?"

"Yeah. Most of it was work related. Business stuff. There were a few personal letters from Brianna, but I didn't glean anything from them. They were mainly chitchat, just keeping me up with family news. There was mention of invitations to visit, which I had apparently declined."

"So it seems as if the caretaker at the cemetery was right—you *had* become a hermit."

"What's a hermit, Mom?" Emma dropped Girl onto the carpet, then sat down while she tugged off her runners.

"Somebody who likes to be alone."

"Unca Jed not a hermit." Jamie shook his head as his mother slipped off his boots. "He likes *us*!"

"You do, don't you, Uncle Jed?" Emma scooped Girl up and, scrambling to her feet, threw Jed an anxious look. "You do like having us here, don't you? We could stay here forever if we wanted to, couldn't we?"

"Yes, sweetie." Jed ruffled her hair affectionately. "You could all stay on here forever if you wanted to. There's nothing I'd like better!"

Emma's face lit up. "Then can we, Mom? Uncle

Jed could find me a school and then next year he could get a place for Jamie in kindergarten and you could stay home all day and look after the new baby.''

"Emma." Sarah frowned at her daughter. "You know how rude it is to invite yourself—''

"It's okay, Sarah," Jed said. "Don't be so hard on her. She's not saying anything I haven't thought about myself."

Sarah ignored him. "Emma, take Jamie and go through to the den. And please stay there till I call you for lunch."

Emma pouted, but she did as she was told.

Sarah waited till they'd left before she said stiffly to Jed, "I'd appreciate if you wouldn't encourage Emma when she talks about staying on."

"I just told her the truth," he retorted. "I'd be happy to have you all stay here—''

"One little white lie wouldn't have hurt!"

"I'm not into lies," he shot back. "White or any other damned color! If there's one thing I consider unforgivable," he added irritably, "it's deceit!"

Unforgivable. The barb tore at Sarah's heart. As she thought of her own ongoing deception, despairing tears welled up in her eyes, tears she didn't want Jed to see. Turning away, she walked blindly toward the den but hadn't gone three steps before he caught her arm and stopped her.

"Sarah." He hauled her around to face him. "The last thing I want to do is upset you." With his thumb pad, he gently brushed a tear from her cheek. "Please don't cry."

Sarah struggled for composure. "I'm not crying…not really. It's just…this is an emotional time…all those hormones running amok…''

He put his arms around her shoulders and pulled her into a comforting embrace. ''I understand. And I'm sorry about backing Emma up—it was unfair. I know you're determined to leave and I should have found a way to avoid answering her question. I guess—'' his tone was wry ''—it was a last-ditch effort on my part to try to get you to change your mind.''

Throat aching, she said, ''I…won't.'' Because I *can't*. ''I do intend leaving, Jed, as soon as the road's passable.''

Jed stood in the bedroom doorway, watching Sarah tuck the children in for the night.

''Good night, Uncle Jed.'' Lying back on her pillow, Emma stuck her thumb in her mouth and waved Girl at him.

Jamie stretched out his arms. ''One more hug, Unca Jed?''

Jed glanced at Sarah and knew by the twinkle in her eyes that she was well aware of Jamie's stalling tactics. He chuckled, and as she moved to the window to close the curtains, he crossed to the bed.

''Hug number five coming up!'' Leaning over, he gave Jamie a hug and dropped a light kiss on his blond crown.

''What about me, Uncle Jed?'' Emma asked.

He kissed her, too, and she sank back with a contented sigh.

''I'm going to miss you,'' she murmured, clutching

Girl to her chest. "But it'll be soooo much fun when you come to visit."

Jed happened to glance at Sarah and was surprised to see an expression of dismay on her face.

As they left the room together, he said quietly, "You have a problem with that?"

"Of course not." She gave a light laugh. "I'm well aware of how irresistible Jamie can be when he wants to stretch out his bedtime. He's a little charmer, isn't he?"

She had deliberately misunderstood his question. Puzzled, Jed tried to figure out why. And why had she appeared to be so dismayed when Emma had talked about his visiting them? Surely it was a given that he was going to keep in touch. Wherever Sarah and her children settled, he wanted to be—intended to be!—a part of their lives. They were family. He wasn't about to let them go. Temporarily, yes. Permanently, no way.

But now wasn't the time to call her on it. He didn't want to risk upsetting her again.

So all he said was, "Yeah, the little guy's a charmer. But what can you expect?" He took her hand and swung it as they walked toward the landing. "He came by it honestly!"

He'd hoped they could spend the rest of the evening together, talking. He wanted to learn more about Sarah—about her relationship with her mother, and with her father before he died. He wanted to know where she'd grown up; what her goals had been before Chance had come onto the scene and screwed up her life. He wanted to know what her dreams were now, what her plans were for her future.

But she seemed determined to thwart him at every turn. When they'd come downstairs after putting the children to bed, he'd offered to help with the dinner dishes, thinking that would provide a good opportunity to chat. But instead she'd said, "Would you mind doing them yourself tonight? I have a load of laundry to sort." Without waiting for an answer, she'd taken off for the laundry room.

When he finished in the kitchen, he'd gone looking for her. He found her coming out of the laundry room. Her face was flushed; her hair wisped damply around her face.

"Ready to sit down?" he asked as they walked to the foyer.

"Shortly." She crossed to the stairs, and as she ascended, she called back, "I want to tidy the children's bathroom first."

By the time she came down again with a bundle of damp towels in her arms, it was almost nine.

He caught her at the foot of the stairs. "What took you so long?"

"While I was up there, I decided I'd get my things gathered together, ready for packing." She smiled brightly at him. "You know I'm not the world's tidiest person. I want to make sure I don't leave anything behind."

"It'll be strange here without you and the kids. The house is going to feel like a morgue." His spirits spiraled downward at the prospect. "You know, Sarah, I can hardly believe you've been here only a matter of days. I feel as if we've known each other forever.''

He thought he saw a shimmer of tears in her eyes, but before he could be sure, she blinked and the shimmer was gone.

''Will you excuse me?'' she said. ''I have some ironing to do.'' She sidestepped him and walked away along the corridor.

She was giving him the brush-off again, dammit! But this time, he wasn't going to let her get away with it.

''I'll keep you company,'' he called after her and saw her falter for a moment before she walked on without answering. He followed her into the laundry room.

She switched on the iron, then opened the dryer door and tugged out a jumble of fresh-smelling laundry, which she dumped on the ironing board. Competently, she began sorting the clothes, folding some, setting some aside for ironing.

''You remind me,'' he said, ''of the Energizer Bunny.''

She threw him a smile, but it didn't reach her eyes. He thought she looked weary and strained.

''Why don't you leave that till morning?'' he asked.

She said, ''No, I'd like to get it out of the way tonight.'' And spreading out one of her shirts, she began ironing it.

He watched her for a long moment and then with an enigmatic ''Mmm,'' he ambled from the room.

Sarah slumped and balancing the iron on its heel, set her hands palms down on the ironing board for support. She'd overdone it, she knew. She should have put her feet up as soon as she'd put the children to bed, but she sensed that Jed wanted to talk with her. And that was something she wanted to avoid.

She didn't want to add to the lies she'd already told him. And so she'd kept herself busy in an effort to keep him at bay. Hoping he'd get the message. And now, she mused with a self-derisive smile, he'd finally gotten it.

Meanwhile, she'd condemned herself to doing a pile of ironing when the only thing she wanted to do was sit down.

Jed sauntered into the room, swinging a kitchen chair from each hand. As she watched, bewildered, he planted the chairs down, facing each other with a space between.

"Sit," he said.

"But I want to do the—"

"You're bushed. But since it seems so damned important to you to get the ironing done tonight, I'll do it."

Sarah could see by the stubborn set of his jaw that he wasn't about to take no for an answer.

"Thank you." She had to force the words out. "I guess if you're determined to do it, I'm not going to fight about it. But I'll go through and sit in the den."

"Uh-uh." He pressed his hand against the small of her back and propelled her to the nearer chair. After seating her, he swung up her legs and rested her feet on the other chair. "You've spent the best part of the evening running away from me. It stops here, Sarah."

She knew when she was beaten.

And she had to admit, albeit reluctantly, that it was

a major relief to be off her feet, whether here or in the den.

What a complex man he was, she reflected as she watched him pick up the iron. A man of such contradictions. The first night they'd met, he'd been a Heathcliff clone—surly, brooding, simmering with dark emotions. Then after his accident, a different man had emerged: a caring, vulnerable man, a man so strong yet so tender he had stolen her heart.

Resting her head on the chair back, she closed her eyes. The room was silent except for the occasional hiss of the iron and its rhythmic thump on the padded ironing board. The sounds were soothing. Restful. Hypnotic...

Jed pressed the tip of the iron around the tiny white buttons on Jamie's blue shirt—the last garment in the pile. Digging his teeth into his lip as he concentrated, he worked the iron with precision over the fine fabric, finishing with the collar, making sure he left no wrinkles.

All done.

He set the iron on its heel, switched it off, folded the shirt and laid it neatly atop the other garments.

As he did, Sarah stirred.

He glanced at her with an indulgent smile. She'd fallen asleep seconds after sitting down; so she had, in the end, thwarted his attempts to have a conversation with her. But that was okay. The last thing he wanted to do was harass her in any way.

All he wanted to do was love her.

Love her?

With shock spreading through him in wild ripples,

he stared at this woman who had crept into his life and had, without his being aware of it, also crept into his heart.

Had not only crept into it, but had stolen it.

He was in love with her....

In love with his brother's widow!

At that moment, Sarah opened her eyes. And after blinking twice, looked up at him with a blank expression. Then she gave him a sheepish smile. "I must have dozed off." Adjusting the folds of her pink-and-white-striped shirt, she added, "Sorry—I guess I wasn't much company."

Unable to keep his eyes off her, he watched as his dazed mind struggled to cope with his newfound love.

"Are you finished?" She put a hand casually over a yawn as she got up and eased her feet into her slippers.

"Yup." He didn't recognize his own voice.

Wrinkling her nose, she said embarrassedly, "I hate people seeing me when I'm sleeping."

"I'm not *people*, Sarah."

She must have heard the intensity in his tone because her reply had an uncharacteristic flippancy that was obviously meant to defuse the moment. "Was my mouth open? Did I snore? Did I look like a beached whale?"

"Sarah," he said urgently, "I have something to tell you."

He saw a flicker of alarm in her eyes before she turned away. With her back to him, she scooped up the ironed clothes. "If you don't mind," she said, "I'd like to go up to bed now." He saw her straighten her shoulders and take in a deep breath before she turned back to him. "I'm really exhausted." She hugged the clothes to her breast like a shield. "Could it wait till tomorrow?"

Jed felt a pang of concern as he looked at her. She *did* look tired. She also looked panicky and agitated, so tightly strung she might snap if pressed further.

"Sure." He looped a reassuring arm around her as he led her to the door. "Of course it can wait till tomorrow."

He could wait, too, because if all went as he hoped—if she could see her way to loving him, as well—they would have many, many tomorrows. And they would spend each and every one of them together.

The prospect filled his heart with joy.

CHAPTER TEN

SARAH woke next morning to the sound of a phone ringing.

She groaned as she realized that the line to the outside world was in order again and she was trapped at Morgan's Hope in the very situation she'd so desperately wanted to avoid. Groggily, she pushed herself up on her elbow—and as she did, the ringing stopped. Jed must have answered it. Was he talking to Brianna...and at this very minute learning of her deception?

With a sense of grim foreboding, she eased her pregnant body off the bed and was on her way to the bathroom when the door burst open. Her heart stopped.

"Mom?"

Just Emma. Her heart galloped into action again.

She turned and saw her daughter in the doorway. "Yes, honey?"

"I was downstairs getting Girl and the phone rang, so I answered it 'cause Uncle Jed's out—he took Max for a walk."

"Who was it?" Sarah held her breath. Please, let it not have been Brianna.

"A man who said to tell Mr. Morgan that the track was already fixed and he could use it any time."

Sarah's breath hissed out. What a dizzying stroke of luck. "Thank you, Emma. But if you hear the phone again, just leave it—it'll be for your uncle and if it's important, the person will call back.''

"Okay, Mom."

"Is Jamie still sleeping?"

"No. Uncle Jed gave us breakfast and then he told us to get dressed and play in our bedroom till you got up."

"Keep an eye on your brother till I have a shower?"

"Sure."

Emma took off and Sarah headed for the bathroom. Now that the phone was in order and the track repaired, chances were that her deception would very soon be uncovered.

Last night, she'd managed to avoid having the talk Jed wanted…though falling asleep in the laundry room hadn't been intentional. But the bedazzled way he'd been staring at her when she woke had shaken her. Was Jed falling in love with her, just as she had fallen for him? If so, it was a love that had no future. A love she knew she mustn't encourage.

So she had deliberately played it cool, acting as if she were oblivious to the urgency and intensity of his tone when he'd said he had something to tell her. But all the time, she was remembering how savagely he'd glared at her the night she'd arrived at Morgan's Hope when she'd told him she'd been married to Chance.

It had been bad enough then, when he'd been a stranger. But now that she was in love with him, the prospect of seeing him look at her in that way again was unbearable.

She had to flee before he came back. If she didn't, she could see this turning into the worst day of her life.

Jed whistled jauntily as he emerged from the forest path with Max at his heels. What a *perfect* day it was. Blue skies, puffy white clouds, bright sunshine. Spring had come to Morgan's Hope at last, and all was well with his world.

He was almost at the front door when it opened and Sarah appeared.

At the sight of him, she stopped short. She had a small case in one hand, a travel bag in the other and a backpack slung over one shoulder.

"Jed!" She sounded breathless. "You're back!"

"What the hell are you doing?"

"Packing the car." She stepped aside to let Emma squeeze by. The child was carting a stack of books. Right behind her was Jamie, puffing as he struggled with a brown paper bag filled to overflowing with toys. As he stumbled, a yellow ball rolled out and fell to the gravel. Max snatched it up and took off.

"Max!" Emma shouted. "Give it here!"

Jed swiveled and looked at the Cutlass. He glowered as he saw that the back seat was already piled high. He swiveled back again. "Sarah—"

"Just let me put these in the car." She threw him a forced-looking smile as she walked past him. "Emma," she called, "not in the back. We'll put these in the trunk."

Jed followed her.

She avoided looking at him as she raised the lid of the trunk. Pushing aside a well-worn infant car seat to make more room, she swung her backpack off and tucked it in a corner. "Emma, put these books here—"

"Sarah, what's your rush? You can't get down the track yet," he added impatiently as she ignored him and packed everything in the trunk. "The road isn't passable!"

Emma tugged his sleeve. "Yes, it is, Uncle Jed. A man phoned and said they finished it early and the road's okay for driving now."

He searched Sarah's face. "The phone lines are up again?"

"Lines are up, track's fixed." She slammed down the trunk lid and turned to him. Her cheeks were pink, the expression in her eyes defensive. "It's all systems go!"

Jamie and Emma had chased away after Max. The loud drone of an approaching helicopter almost drowned out their laughter as they ran around the forecourt trying to catch up with the Lab, who still had Jamie's ball between his teeth.

Jed could feel his family slipping away from him. But he wasn't about to let that happen.

"Sarah, wait." He put a hand on her shoulder as she would have walked away. "Dammit, woman, I want to talk to you—"

"I won't change my mind." The breeze gusted up her shirt and she pressed it down again with her palms. "I've loved being at Morgan's Hope—you've been so good to us all. But it's time to go. I don't want to outstay my welcome."

"That could never happen." Jed took her hands in his, held them tightly. "Sarah, last night—"

He broke off as the ever-increasing roar of the helicopter made his words inaudible. He took in a frustrated breath, glancing up at the sky as he prepared to wait till he could be heard. What he had to say demanded Sarah's complete and undivided attention.

The chopper was descending, the noise of its engines more deafening by the moment. It wasn't till Jed saw it hover above the clearing where his cabin was situated that he realized that that was apparently its destination.

And at the same moment, he remembered the notation on the kitchen calendar: MINERVA LEAVING. Today was the last day of the month. Mitch had come to pick up the sculpture.

The timing couldn't have been worse.

Sarah slipped her hands from his grasp and raised them to her brow, cupping them over her eyes as she followed the choppper's path. Her blond hair shimmered, the ends fluttering against her neck. He wanted to frame her face in his hands and kiss her till she could hardly draw breath.

Instead, he just touched her arm.

She jerked her head around to look at him, and he shouted, "He's come to get the sculpture."

After a blank second, understanding dawned in her eyes. She nodded and mouthed, "*Minerva*."

"I'll have to help," he yelled.

She nodded again.

"Don't go anywhere!" He grimaced as he realized he had shouted into sudden silence. The chopper had landed; the pilot had cut the engine. "Don't go anywhere," he repeated in a normal voice, fixing Sarah with a warning gaze. "We'll talk when I get back. Okay?"

"I'll be here," she said.

"Promise?"

"Promise."

"Good." He turned away and strode across the forecourt and a moment later had disappeared into the forest.

Feeling as if her heart was breaking, Sarah watched him leave.

"But why couldn't we wait and say goodbye to Uncle Jed, Mom?"

Sarah's vision was half-blurred with tears. If only she could stop crying! Brushing a trembling hand over her eyes, she kept the other on the steering wheel as she drove the Cutlass along the highway toward Vancouver. "Emma—"

A gasp escaped her as an overwhelming pain clutched her middle. It held tight for a few seconds and then, to her relief, it let go.

She fought off a feeling of apprehension. It must be indigestion. She'd rushed her morning milk she'd been in such a hurry to leave. She *wasn't* going into labor yet. Couldn't be. It was just another false alarm. Had to be.

"Mom?" Emma's querulous voice drifted from the back seat. "I said, why—"

"I have very good reasons, reasons you're too young to understand." Sarah forced herself to concentrate on her driving as a huge rig overtook her. "I want you to sit there quietly with Jamie—"

At mention of his name, Jamie started to cry—the high keening wail he adopted only when he was truly distressed.

Sarah felt the grating sound scrape on her bruised nerves. "Hush, Jamie, everything's going to be fine."

His wailing intensified. "I want Max!"

"Play with your puzzle." She raised her voice over the din. "Emma, read your books, or—"

"I wanna know where we're going!" Emma demanded in her most aggressive tone. "Why did we have to leave Uncle Jed? I don't wanna leave him and I don't wanna leave Max! Besides," she added belligerently, "I heard you promise Uncle Jed you'd stay so he could talk to you. And you've always told us we must keep a promise if we make one!"

Sarah swallowed over a raw lump in her throat. "Please, Emma. I don't want to discuss it."

The pain came again. This time, it was much stronger; she felt as if her insides were being twisted by a giant hand. She tensed, tried not to give in to her fear.

Gradually, the pain eased. Leaving her shaken.

After a while, Jamie's cries became less strident and eventually tailed off to a low, intermittent wail.

Emma had become quiet.

When Sarah checked in the rearview mirror, she saw that her daughter's face was flushed and her thumb was stuck firmly in her mouth, Girl clutched against her neck. The child was staring out the side window with mutinous eyes.

Sarah sighed. Emma had asked where they were going but she couldn't answer her question because she didn't *know* where they were going. When she'd fled Morgan's Hope, she hadn't thought the matter through. In her panic, all she'd cared about was getting away before Jed came back.

And now, here they all were, with little money in the bank, a baby who seemed impatient to make its entry into the world…

And no place to call home.

Sarah shivered. And all of a sudden, she felt clammy and filled with dread…the kind of feeling a person might get if she stepped into a dank, dark cellar.

Or through the front doors of Wynthrop. That beautiful mansion just an hour's drive away, where she'd been born and brought up. The house where she was no longer welcome.

Wynthrop was the last place in the world she'd take Emma and Jamie…if she had a choice.

But she realized something now that she'd shoved to the darkest reaches of her mind for weeks: she *had* no choice. No matter how she'd denied it to herself, she'd known that in the end she had only one place where she could go.

She had to return home. She had to ask her mother to let her stay there with the children till after her baby was born.

The Cutlass was gone.

Jed came to an abrupt halt and stared in disbelief at the deserted forecourt. He stood for an endless moment, the only sound he could hear the frantic thrumming of his heart.

Then he sprang to life and ran to the house. As he reached the front door, it hit him like a bolt from the blue that he hadn't run like this since the night of the fire—

Memories. He froze with his hand on the doorknob

as memories flashed before his eyes, each separate memory like a piece of a jigsaw puzzle, incomplete on its own and with no big picture to see where each piece fitted in. He felt dizzy as one image or sensation after another flaunted itself for an instant, giving him no time to sort them all out.

Flames, leaping to a purple-dark sky. The ear-piercing wail of a siren. The pungent smell of burning wood—

As abruptly as they'd started, the memories stopped. Leaving him feeling sick and shaken.

Trying to get a grip on himself, he shoved the door open and went inside. Looking with despair around the empty foyer, he shouted, "Sarah?" But as his voice echoed back from upstairs, he knew it was hopeless. She had gone.

But still, some stubborn part of him refused to give up hope. He had to make *sure*.

He searched the main floor. Not one sign of her. He took the stairs to the landing three steps at a time and then raced from bedroom to bedroom to bedroom.

Nobody. Nothing.

He ended up in Sarah's bathroom. And there at last he found a trace of her—a hint of her perfume in the air, a sheen of moisture on the walls from her shower.

Clenching his fists, he stared at his reflection in the mirror. "I'll find her," he swore aloud, "if it's the last thing I ever do."

Jaw clamped determinedly, he turned to go. And that's when he noticed her robe.

It was hanging on a hook on the back of the bath-room door. In her haste to leave, she'd apparently forgotten it. He reached for the pink flannel garment and, crushing it in his hands, buried his face in the soft, Sarah-scented fabric. He stood that way for a long moment, breathing in the essence of her, anguish overflowing his heart.

Finally, he exhaled a deep breath and straightened. For heaven's sake, he was acting like a moonstruck adolescent! If he wanted to find the woman he loved, he'd better *do* something instead of wallowing in self-pity.

Irritated with himself, he made to hang the robe back on the hook. And heard paper crackle in one of the pockets.

He slid his hand into the folds and drew out an envelope. To his puzzlement, he saw it was addressed to him and the return address was Brianna's.

How the hell had it come into Sarah's possession? he wondered. And why on earth had she hidden it from him?

He read the letter. Once, twice. And as the truth of it finally sank in, his head began to pound. Memories again flickered into his mind, vivid and powerful memories, pieces of the jigsaw. But this time, they didn't stop. And before very long, he knew he was in possession of every piece.

The jigsaw of his past was complete.

Wynthrop looked even more imposing, more intimidating, than Sarah had remembered it to be.

But despite her trepidation, she acknowledged as she spun the Cutlass along the rhododendron-lined drive that it was a welcome sight.

For the last few miles of her journey, her contractions had become so severe she'd almost had to pull over to the shoulder of the highway. But drawing on a deep well of strength, she'd managed to keep going with only one goal in mind: to get to Wynthrop before she lost control.

Skidding the car to a halt in the forecourt, she felt an overwhelming shudder of relief. But on the heels of her relief came another wave of pain.

She moaned as it took over—and spared a moment to be thankful the children had earlier fallen asleep. She rode with the contraction, which seemed to go on forever, and then, when it started to slacken, she saw the front door open.

Dread sent adrenaline rushing through her. But it wasn't her mother who appeared after all. It was Mariah, the housekeeper. Gray-haired and sturdy, the woman stood on the top step, peering at the unfamiliar vehicle.

Sarah opened the car door and levered her bulky body out of the seat. She heard Mariah cry, "Sarah!" but the housekeeper's smile changed to a frown of concern when Sarah gasped and hunched over at the onset of another contraction.

The housekeeper ran over to her. "Sarah, honey, what's wrong?"

"Look after Emma and Jamie, will you, please, Mariah?" Sarah gasped as another wave of pain hit her. "But first..." She clutched Mariah's hands. "Help me into the house and call an ambulance."

The next couple of hours passed in a blur.

Sarah wondered afterward if she would ever remember any of it clearly. But one thing she did remember—and knew she always would—was the moment the doctor placed her baby in her arms and said in a cheerful voice, "Well done, Sarah Morgan. You have a beautiful and healthy baby girl."

Jed paced the kitchen over and over and over again.

Chance had been responsible for the fire that killed Jeralyn. He could still scarcely believe it.

And how long had Sarah known?

Had she known it when she turned up here the night of the storm? Or had she learned about it from the cashier who'd told her how Jeralyn had died? Or had she found out only when she'd read Brianna's letter?

And how had the letter come into her possession? He was pretty damned sure he knew the answer to *that* question. She must have come on it the night they'd worked together, going through the box of paperwork he'd brought over from the cabin. He remembered now how guilty she'd looked when he'd disturbed her next morning—she'd been deeply immersed in a letter when he'd pushed open the study door. She must have tucked it back in her pile and then crept down to appropriate it and hide it from him before he got up.

He needed to find her. He intended to find her. No matter how long it took. And it might take a very long time indeed, considering how little he had to go on.

But first, he had to get himself a vehicle.

He phoned for a cab to take him into Kentonville, then he went upstairs and packed an overnight bag.

Wherever you are, Sarah Morgan, he thought

grimly, I'll find you. We have some unfinished business, you and I.

"Mom." Emma ran tearfully into Sarah's bedroom and across to her mother. "I don't like Grandma!"

Sarah was sitting on a low chair by the window, her three-day-old baby cradled in her arms. The infant paid no heed to Emma, just kept sucking Sarah's nipple. It was a wonder, Sarah thought, that her milk hadn't dried up, considering the stress she'd been under since the birth.

She pulled Emma close. "Grandma's been very kind, letting us stay here. I know it's difficult for you, getting used to her...but it's hard for her, too, having you and Jamie running around her nice house."

"Jamie didn't *mean* to break her best mice dish—"

"Meissen, honey. No, of course he didn't. It was an accident—"

"Well, *you* don't ever put us in our room when it's just an accident!" For the moment, indignation overcame Emma's unhappiness. "And you would *never* give us a time-out for breaking a silly old plate!"

Sarah said, "It was a very expensive plate, sweetie." As the baby released her nipple, she propped the precious bundle against her shoulder and burped her. "Is Jamie asleep?"

"Yes." Emma's lower lip jutted out in a pout. "And I've got nobody to play with!" Her lip trembled ominously as she added, "*And* Grandma says I have to go to the store with her 'cause she says my clothes are ugly—"

"Emma—" Deirdre Hallston's autocratic voice

preceded her "—I told you not to disturb your mother."

Sarah braced herself as her mother walked through the doorway. Deirdre Hallston had always been a clotheshorse, and today her model-slim figure was elegantly attired in a black linen suit and high-heeled black pumps of the finest quality. Her platinum hair was drawn back in a chignon to reveal the flawless cut of her patrician features. And her winter-gray eyes, fixed on Emma, were hard with disapproval.

"I told you, Emma, to wash your face and hands." Her mouth tightened. "Please do so now."

Sarah kissed Emma and gave her a comforting hug. "Honey, off you go. It'll be fun, shopping with Grandma. And lovely to buy some new outfits!"

Emma flashed her mother a scornful look that made Sarah feel like a traitor, then twisting from her mother's embrace, the child ran from the room.

Sarah thought she heard a gulping sob.

And her anger at her mother intensified.

"Emma doesn't need new clothes, Mother. In future, please tell me of your plans before arranging anything with the children."

"As long as you're staying at Wynthrop," her mother snapped, "your children will not run around in cheap little outfits. I'm sure you will recall that when you were a child, you wore the best that money could buy. You wanted for nothing! And if you hadn't been so set on marrying that no-good, moneygrubbing Morgan boy, I'd have seen to it that Emma had exactly the same privileged childhood—"

"Please don't talk like that about Chance. He's—"

"Dead. Yes, I know that only too well since he left

you penniless! If he'd managed to provide for you, you wouldn't have needed to come crawling home.''

Her raised voice brought a whimper from the baby.

Sarah got to her feet. ''Yes.'' She crossed to the changing table. ''I *did* come crawling home. But only because I had nowhere else to go. I know I'm not welcome here, and as soon as I'm able, I'll leave. In the meantime, all I ask is that you try to be kind to Jamie and Emma. They've gone through a lot the past few months—''

''You could have made it easier for them,'' her mother said tersely, ''if you had come here right after your husband died, instead of going to his brother!'' A frown of displeasure marred her brow. ''You've refused to tell me one thing about the man, so I have to assume that you found him just as irresponsible as his brother was since you didn't stay with him very long!''

''He's not irresponsible.'' Sarah gently placed the baby on the changing table. ''He's kind and reliable and—''

Her mother's contemptuous snort made Sarah see red.

''—he's a *wonderful* man.'' She snatched a diaper from the shelf under the table. ''And I'm in *love* with him.'' Defiantly, she glared at her mother.

Deirdre Hallston stared back at her with a look of horror. And then slowly, very slowly, she shook her head. ''My God,'' she said incredulously, ''you just never learn, do you? Well, missy, you say you're planning to leave here once you feel strong enough…'' She inhaled deeply, her nostrils quivering as she did. ''But I'll tell you one thing. When you do, you'll leave here alone. You've just admitted that your children have been through a terrible upheaval—well, it's high time they started living in a stable environment. I wouldn't be doing my duty if I allowed you to take them away from here. The very fact that you've let yourself become involved with another of these Morgan men is blatant proof that you're an unfit mother!''

''Don't you dare say—''

''Oh, I dare.'' Her mother whirled away. Over her shoulder, she said harshly, ''I'll fight in the courts if I have to...but I wouldn't be doing my duty as a grandmother if I didn't take these poor children out of your hands!''

CHAPTER ELEVEN

JED stared with dismay at the JD Electronics building as he drew his spanking-new Nissan Pathfinder to a halt in the visitors' parking lot. This company looked bigger than any of those he'd visited in the past three days and would surely employ hundreds of people.

His search for Sarah's mother was becoming more hopeless by the minute. It wasn't surprising, of course. All he knew about her was that she was a widow and worked in an administrative capacity at one of Vancouver's top electronics firms.

He didn't let himself dwell on the fact that he might be on a wild-goose chase—the woman had disowned her own daughter, and if he found her, she might well turn him away, too. But it was worth a try. Sarah had told him she planned to contact an old friend after leaving Morgan's Hope; he hoped her mother would know who her friends were and pass on the information.

He strode into the building and was directed to the personnel department, where he was greeted by a silver-haired woman with a friendly expression.

"How may I help you?" she asked.

He went into the same spiel he'd given over and over again in all the other offices he'd visited. "I'm trying to track down a friend," he said, "through her mother. I don't know much about the mother except that she was widowed about sixteen years ago, and

her job's in electronics. My friend's name is Sarah—
Sarah Morgan.''

The woman shook her head. ''No, it doesn't ring
a bell. It's a big company, of course, but I've worked
here since it started up, and being in personnel I know
everybody...and everybody's family problems, too!''

Another dead end. Jed forced a smile. ''Thanks,''
he said. ''I knew it was a long shot.''

''Why do you need to find this woman? Oh, I'm
not being nosy,'' she added. ''It's just that I have lots
of contacts in this business and I can make a few
calls, try to track her down. The more I know, the
better my chances will be.''

''It's not really relevant,'' Jed said, hiding his reluctance to divulge more. ''Sarah—her daughter—
and I have some unfinished business. Even if I can
find the mother,'' he said, ''she may not give me the
information I need. She threw her daughter out six
years ago—the girl was pregnant and determined to
marry the baby's father, against her mother's
wishes.''

''Oh, my!'' The woman's eyes widened. ''It's little
Sarah you're looking for! Good heavens above!''

Jed gripped the counter. ''You *know* her? You
know where I can find her mother?''

''Her office is up in the penthouse—but she's not
in today,'' she called as Jed made to leave. ''She's at
home.''

''*Where can I find her*?''

''She lives outside the city...14 Pinetree Trail. I
can tell you where it is exactly because I was there
on the day of her husband's funeral. Follow the highway till you reach Pinetree Mall, then turn right and

go straight for about two miles. The house is the last one on the left.''

Jed cruised slowly along Pinetree Trail, whistling in awe as he saw the enormous houses on either side, each set in a few acres of land. The grounds were immaculately landscaped, the houses themselves more like castles than homes.

How did Sarah's mother fit in here? he wondered. Did she rent a cottage on someone's property? An apartment above a garage? A basement suite?

He slowed at the end of the street, then guided his vehicle through the gateway of number 14. He didn't get a full view of the house till he'd emerged from the rhododendron-lined drive, and when he did, he realized that of all the mansions on Pinetree Trail, this was by far the most stunning. Its gardens, too, were magnificent—a Technicolor glory of spring flowers and shrubs.

He followed the drive to the side of the house, where he parked in an inconspicuous spot. While he searched for Sarah's mother, he didn't want to put her on the spot by intruding on the owner of the "big house."

He let the Pathfinder door click shut quietly, then shoving his hands into the hip pockets of his jeans, he walked cautiously to the back of the house.

He glanced around but saw no cottage; and the four-car garage was a single story, so Sarah's mother couldn't live—

"He's *not* irresponsible."

From above, the familiar voice floated to his ears. Jed stopped in his tracks.

"He's kind and reliable and—he's a *wonderful* man." Sarah sounded angry, defiant. "And I'm..."

Her voice became muffled; he couldn't make out what she said. But his heartbeats took off in a crazy race even as profound satisfaction rippled through him. He had found her. Dammit, he had actually found her. And much more easily than he'd expected.

But...where *exactly* was she?

He looked up and saw an open window. She was in there? What the devil was she doing in this fancy house?

Scratching his head in puzzlement, he heard snatches of another voice. A voice that was so cold and disapproving it gave him goose bumps.

"...never learn, do you? Well, missy, you say...planning to leave...when you do...leave here alone...I wouldn't be doing my duty if...proof that you're an unfit mother!"

Then Sarah's voice again. An outraged protest.

Jed knew he ought not to be listening. But he couldn't move. And as he leaned against the wall, he heard the woman—Sarah's mother undoubtedly—warn that she'd stop at nothing to get custody of her grandchildren.

He heard the sound of a door being slammed, and as he did, he straightened. That witch, he promised himself grimly, would get Sarah's children over his dead body. And he wasn't about to waste one minute before telling her so.

He hammered on the back door and it was opened by a middle-aged woman in a black dress and snow-white apron. Her expression was strained.

"My name's Jed Morgan," he announced without

preamble, ready to thrust his foot in the doorway if necessary. ''I want to see Sarah.''

The woman hesitated. ''I'll have to talk with Mrs. Hallston—''

''Mrs. Hallston? What the heck does she have to do with—''

''You're Chance's brother?''

Jed's eyes narrowed. ''That's right.''

The woman threw a nervous glance over her shoulder and when she spoke again it was in a tight whisper. ''She won't want Sarah to see you. She doesn't want her daughter to have anything more to do with your family.''

It took a moment for the penny to drop, but when it did, Jed gawked at the servant. ''Are you telling me that Sarah is—that Sarah's a Hallston?''

''Well, yes…of course.''

''And her mother…?''

''Mrs. Hallston is the owner of JD Electronics.''

Jed felt punch-drunk. Unbelievable. Sarah had never given him the first clue that she came from such a wealthy background. ''She…Sarah…lived in this house?''

''Born and brought up here.'' The woman leaned toward him and said quietly, ''Her father's daughter. He was a dear, sweet man. After his death, Sarah was never the same. She always seemed to be…searching…for something.''

Searching for a family.

Guilt slammed Jed in the gut. She'd come to Morgan's Hope hoping that there, at last, she'd find a home. The kind of home she dreamed of. Instead, he'd thrown her out. Just as her mother had six years before.

"Mr. Morgan, why do you want to see Sarah?"

"I intend to give her that something," he said, "that she's been searching for."

The woman beamed. Stepping back, she gestured for him to enter. "I may lose my job over this," she whispered. "But if you can make Sarah happy, it'll be worth it."

She ushered him out of the kitchen and along to a lavishly furnished foyer. A curving mahogany staircase led up to a gallery.

"Sarah's room is upstairs," she said in his ear. "At the far end of the corridor." She patted his arm. "Good luck."

Jed met no one as he ascended the stairs, met no one as he strode along the carpeted corridor. When he reached the door at the far end, he found it ajar.

He tapped it lightly, but when he got no answer, he pushed it open. From behind a door to his left, he heard the sound of running water. And then…he heard another sound.

A baby's whimper.

That's when he saw the white crib tucked in a corner of the room, close to the bed. Heard another faint murmur coming from it.

His heart trembled. Dear God, Sarah had had her baby.

He stood for a long moment, letting the sheer joy of it wash over him.

Then holding his breath, he walked on tiptoes across the plush carpet and peeked into the crib.

The blankets were pink, the first intimation that the

baby was a girl. And when he looked at the infant, he saw that her cheeks were also pink, her tiny face round, her skin like silk. Her dark eyes were wide open and appeared to be staring up at him with frank curiosity.

He felt as if he was looking at a miracle. Rosebud mouth, tiny fingernails, dainty ears, wispy blond hair. In her sugar-pink sleeper, she was out-of-this-world glorious.

As he gazed at her in wonderment, a spasm of discomfort suddenly crossed her features. The rosebud mouth turned down. She started to cry. A cry that within seconds became shrill and demanding.

Jed brushed back the covers and, holding his breath again, lifted her in his arms. She was light as thistledown and dearer than life itself. And, as he looked at her through a shining blur of tears, he wondered if it was possible for a heart to break if it was exposed to too much happiness.

If there was one thing Sarah hated, it was self-pity! With an angry hand, she rubbed her facecloth over her cheeks, hard, to scrub away the tears she'd shed after her mother had stalked out and slammed the door.

There was no way she'd let Deidre Hallston take her children from her. She wasn't sure yet how she'd stop her—her mind was in too much of a muddle— but as soon as she got her strength back, she'd think of something. It was just so hard to cope with thoughts of tomorrow when she was missing Jed so much she could hardly cope with today.

Choking back a sob, she dropped the cloth and

picked up her hairbrush. After brushing the tangles from her hair, she swept it back and was about to gather it with a ribbon when she heard the baby cry.

She paused and listened. Was it wind? Or was the little sweetie just whimpering in her sleep?

The cry became shrill and demanding. And then it stopped. Abruptly.

That was unusual....

Quickly, Sarah put down the brush, opened the bathroom door...

And froze. Incredulous. Stunned. Dizzy. Wondering if she wasn't awake after all but lost in a world of dreams, because there, in the corner of her bedroom, stood...Jed.

He was cradling the baby, holding her as carefully as if she was the most precious thing he'd ever seen.

"Jed...?" The word came out on a shaky breath.

He looked up—and her heart faltered when she saw the tears in his eyes. "Hi," he said. He brushed a kiss over the infant's wispy blond hair before laying her gently back in the crib and covering her lightly with her pink blanket.

"Wh-what are you doing here?" Sarah's voice was so thin and thready she didn't recognize it.

He smiled, and the smile did very odd things to her heart.

"My memory came back," he said. "I know everything. And I've come to take you home."

"T-take me h-home?" Sarah stuttered. "B-but I thought you wouldn't want me around to remind you of Chance—and I thought you'd despise me because I deceived you."

"Sweetheart, the only person I despised was myself when I remembered the way I treated you when you arrived at Morgan's Hope. Sure, you'd been married to Chance, but you were in no way responsible for the tragedy—and I treated you as if you were. It boggles my mind that I was going to throw you and the kids out—''

''Oh, Jed, don't be so hard on yourself. You were still dealing with the past, with your loss, and with Chance's part in it.''

''It's over now.'' His eyes were dark with emotion. ''But it might never have been if you hadn't come to Morgan's Hope. My anger and bitterness had made me cut myself off from life. Jeralyn and I had been so happy together—and I'd lost her. I wasn't about to open myself up to a repeat of that kind of heartbreak. But with the past wiped from my mind and no longer acting as a barrier, I opened myself up and I fell in love again. When my memory came back, Sarah, I realized how much I might have forfeited if I hadn't given love another chance.'' He walked steadily over to her and took her in his arms. ''I just feel so grateful that you came into my life when you did.''

''Oh, Jed.'' A tear trembled on Sarah's eyelashes.

Jed brushed it tenderly away. And then with a smile, he looked over at the crib. ''You've been busy,'' he said huskily, ''since I last saw you.''

''Isn't she adorable?'' Sarah felt a rush of love as she followed his gaze. ''She arrived just hours after I left the mountain!''

''Have you named her yet?''

''I was thinking of you when I chose her name.''

She smiled through a mist of tears. "I called her…Hope."

"Hope," he murmured. "I like that." He held her close against his heart. "I've missed you." His voice held a thread of pain. "So damned much."

For a long moment, she just nestled into his embrace, savoring his warmth, his rhythmic breathing, his familiar male scent. She'd fantasized about such a moment, never once believing it could happen.

She looked up at him and gloried in the happiness she saw in his eyes. Reaching up, with loving fingers she threaded back the swath of black hair that had fallen over his brow. "It took you long enough to get here!"

"Have you any idea," he growled, "how hard it is to track someone down when all you know is that her mother works in an electronics firm? It would have been a helluva lot easier if I'd known your mother owned her own company. You're one secretive wench, Sarah Morgan."

"From now on, Jed, there'll be no more secrets. Like you, I hate deception." She bit her lip. "I forgot my robe—I guess you found it, with Brianna's letter in the pocket? Did you finally get in touch with her?"

"I did. I tracked her down through the Nick and Allie Campbell she'd mentioned in that first letter— thank heavens *they* didn't have an unlisted number! When I called her, she told me she and her husband, Harry, had tried their best during the past few years to draw me out of my depression. She was delighted to learn that I was in good form again and chasing after the woman I wanted to marry."

Sarah took in a deep breath. "Jedidiah Morgan…is that a proposal?"

He faked a look of surprise. "Wow…well, yeah. I guess it is!"

She laughed. "Then," she said, "I guess I'll accept. But you do know we come as a package? Take one, take all?"

"Sounds like a deal to me!" he said. "And from where I stand, it's a bargain."

She blushed. "Jed, do you remember promising not to kiss me again…but that if I ever felt a pressing need to kiss you, you would cooperate?"

He cocked a teasing brow. "Am I to understand that you are feeling such a pressing need right now?"

Her blush deepened. "Actually," she murmured, "I've been feeling it almost constantly, from the moment you gave me that bone-melting kiss when you came home from hospital."

"Bone-melting, huh?" His eyes twinkled.

"But I thought you were just trying to sweeten me up so that I'd stay and look after you. Then later on, when we'd become friends and you suggested we might end up falling in love, I decided to keep my distance and give you the brush-off because I thought that when your memory came back you'd hate me again."

"We've wasted a helluva lot of time, Sarah Morgan. But I'm not about to stand here wasting any more. So if you're serious about this pressing need to kiss me—"

"Oh," she said breathlessly, "I'm serious."

"Then you shall have my full cooperation."

His lips were on hers almost before he'd finished

speaking. And the kiss more than made up for all the time they'd wasted. Sarah thought she might swoon with the bliss of it. By the time they drew apart, her legs could hardly support her. "Wow," she whispered, "that was well worth the wait."

"And that," he said with a sexy smile, "was just a sample of what's ahead. I can hardly wait to get you home."

Sarah relaxed into his embrace. "Jamie and Emma will be thrilled to hear the news. They've been so miserable here, Jed. My mother—"

"I heard your mother." Jed shook his head. "I was walking around the side of the house and your window was open. I can understand why you didn't want to come here—you must have been desperate. I'll never forgive myself for—"

"Jed, there's nothing to forgive. We're together now, and that's all that matters."

"You're right." He dropped a kiss on her brow. "So how long will it take for you to gather your things—"

"Sarah!" Deirdre Hallston's voice was shrill with outrage. "What is that man doing in your bedroom?"

Sarah was glad of Jed's arm around her as she turned to face her mother. Deirdre Hallston's cheeks were scarlet with anger. But when she caught her first glimpse of Jed's face, the color swiftly drained away. She gasped, then put a hand to her throat.

It was obvious to Sarah that her mother had thought she was looking at a ghost. Chance's ghost.

"This is Jed Morgan, Mother." She tilted her chin determinedly. "Jed has just asked me to marry him."

Her mother's eyes turned flinty hard. "You are making one big mistake, missy, if you—"

"I've said yes."

In the silence that followed Sarah's quiet statement, she felt Jed's arm tighten around her.

"Good girl," he murmured. "Way to go, sweetheart!"

As she leaned against him, she heard the pitter-patter of footsteps scurrying along the corridor and then Emma and Jamie ran headlong into the bedroom.

When they saw Jed, they skidded to a halt. Their eyes were wide with disbelief. Emma was the first to recover from her surprise.

"Uncle Jed!" she screamed, then hurled herself at him.

Jamie shouted, "Unca Jed!" and hurled himself after his sister.

Jed released Sarah and with a wide smile swept them both up off their feet. They hung around his neck, and he looped his arms around their bottoms as they showered him with fervent kisses.

When he finally dropped them to the carpet, they commandeered his hands and clung as if they'd never let go. Staring up at him adoringly, they pounded him with questions. "How come you're here? Are you staying? How's Max?"

When he managed to get a word in edgewise, he said, "Max is fine. He's missed you all, and so have I. So I've come to take you all home with me."

They screamed with delight.

When at last Jed looked up to see how Deirdre Hallston was reacting to what was going on, he discovered she'd gone.

His eyes met Sarah's. "Gather up your things," he said. "And be as fast as you can. I want to get you and the kids out of here."

It took just fifteen minutes to pack and then they carried everything downstairs and out to his vehicle.

Sarah looked at the Pathfinder. "Did you rent this?"

"Bought it in Kentonville."

"It's cool, Uncle Jed!" Emma grinned as she clambered up into the vehicle. "And just the right size for a family."

"That's why I bought it, honeybunch!"

"You were pretty sure of yourself, weren't you?" Sarah said with mock indignation.

He grinned. "Positive thinking," he said. "It works wonders."

"I'm not going to argue with that," Sarah said with a laugh. "Now we'll need to transfer the infant seat and Jamie's car seat from the Cutlass. What are we going to do about my car?"

"I'll arrange to have it towed to a used-car lot," Jed said. "No way is my wife going drive an old junker!"

After everything was stowed away and the children safely belted in, Jed said to Sarah, "Are you going to say goodbye to your mother?"

With a feeling of sorrow, Sarah shook her head. "No," she said. "She doesn't want to see me."

She knew that after this day she would never come back to Wynthrop. For years she'd harbored, in a rarely visited corner of her heart the secret hope that her mother, deep down, did love her. She no longer harbored that hope. Deirdre Hallston was a cold woman who didn't have the capacity to love.

The knowledge was like a dark cloud spoiling her joy. Jed must have sensed it because he leaned across and brushed a kiss over her cheek. "Hang in there," he murmured. "This, too, shall pass."

She managed a smile, but as she sank back in her seat, she knew that though the pain of rejection might eventually become dull, it would never totally go away.

"Mom," Emma cried, "I forgot Girl!"

Jed turned his head and looked at her. "Run back and get her, honey. We'll wait."

"I think I left her in the solarium. I don't wanna go back there." Emma scowled. "Grandma'll be there."

Sarah stifled a sigh. "I'll get it."

Jed said, "I'll go."

She shook her head. "It's okay."

The house was quiet as Sarah entered the foyer. And her steps were quiet as she walked over the Aubusson carpet.

The solarium door was ajar.

She made no sound as she pushed it open.

Yes, her mother was there. But the sight that met Sarah's eyes stopped her as abruptly as if she'd walked into a wall.

Deirdre Hallston was sitting slackly on a high-backed chair with Emma's doll pressed to her breast and an expression of utter desolation etched on her face.

Stunned, Sarah uttered an involuntary sound of dismay.

Her mother straightened abruptly and jerked her head around.

When she saw Sarah, her eyes flared wide—for just a fraction of a second—then she clamped her features into a tight mask and closed off her rawly exposed emotions.

''You came back for this.'' Her voice rasped between them. Stiff as a robot, she rose and held out the doll.

Mother and daughter stood looking at each other, the atmosphere crowded with words unsaid. Everything in Deirdre Hallston's demeanor warned Sarah that her mother would never admit to the lonely despair that had swamped her as she sat alone, waiting for her daughter to leave.

And Sarah was not about to humiliate her mother by calling her on it. Instead, she took the doll and said softly, ''Jed's a good man, Mother. And now…he's family. You're welcome to come visit us at any time.''

Her mother's mouth worked, but she said nothing.

Sarah felt sadness envelop her. If this were fiction, her mother would by now have reached out and opened her arms to her only child. But there had never been any physical contact between them. It was too late, surely, to expect that now.

She turned away, walking with heavy steps across the solarium and through the foyer. But as she emerged from the house into the sunny afternoon, she heard her mother call after her.

''Perhaps—'' the voice was strained ''—you might send me an invitation to your wedding.''

Sarah turned and, through the open doorway, saw

her mother standing in the middle of the foyer. With a sense of shock, she noticed that Deirdre Hallston looked frail and, for the first time, every day her age.

"Yes." Sarah's eyes misted. "I will."

When she returned to the car, Jed was standing by the passenger side, his hand on the roof. He raised his eyebrows in question. "What took you so long? Problems?"

"No." She tossed Girl into Emma's eager hands. "But I'll tell you all about it later." Slipping down into her seat, she looked up at him, her unclouded happiness spilling over in a joyous smile.

"In the meantime," she said, "let's go home."

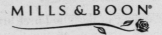

Enjoy a romantic novel from
Mills & Boon®

Presents...™ *Enchanted*™ TEMPTATION.

Historical Romance™ ◢MEDICAL ROMANCE®

Hiring
Ms. Right

Three single women, one home–help agency—and three professional bachelors in search of...a wife?

⭐ Are you a busy executive with a demanding career?

⭐ Do you need help with those time-consuming everyday errands?

⭐ Ever wished you could hire a house-sitter, caterer...or even a glamorous partner for that special social occasion?

*Meet **Cassie, Sabrina** and **Paige**—three independent women who've formed a business taking care of those troublesome domestic crises.*

And meet the three gorgeous bachelors who are simply looking for a little help...and instead discover they've hired Ms Right!

Enjoy bestselling author **Leigh Michaels's** new trilogy:

HUSBAND ON DEMAND—March 2000
BRIDE ON LOAN—May 2000
WIFE ON APPROVAL—July 2000

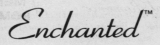

COMING NEXT MONTH

MILLS & BOON®

Enchanted™

THE OUTBACK AFFAIR by Elizabeth Duke

Natasha was horrified when her tour guide turned out to be Tom Scanlon—the man who'd once jilted her. It was too intimate a situation for ex-lovers—but Tom wanted Natasha back. And now he had two weeks alone with her to prove just how much!

THE BEST MAN AND THE BRIDESMAID
by Liz Fielding

As chief bridesmaid, Daisy is forced out of her usual shapeless garb and into a beautiful dress. Suddenly the best man, determinedly single Robert Furneval, whom she has always loved, begins to see her in a whole new light…

HUSBAND ON DEMAND by Leigh Michaels

Jake Abbott has arrived at his brother's house—to discover that Cassie has been hired to look after the residence. He's clearly very happy for their temporary living arrangements to become more intimate. But what about permanent…?

THE FEISTY FIANCÉE by Jessica Steele

When Yanice fell for her boss, Thomson Wakefield, she adhered to her belief that love means marriage, but did it mean the same for him? A near tragic accident brings her answer, but can Yanice trust the proposal of a man under heavy sedation?

Available from 3rd March 2000

Available at most branches of WH Smith, Tesco, Martins,
Borders, Easons, Volume One/James Thin
and most good paperback bookshops

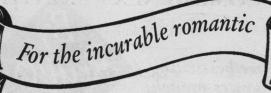

MILLS & BOON®

*Three bestselling
romances brought
back to you by
popular demand*

By Request™

Latin Lovers

The Heat of Passion *by Lynne Graham*
Carlo vowed to bring Jessica to her knees,
however much she rejected him. But now she
faced a choice: three months in Carlo's bed, or
her father would go to jail.

The Right Choice *by Catherine George*
When Georgia arrived in Italy to teach English
to little Alessa, she was unprepared for her uncle,
the devastating Luca. Could she resist?

Vengeful Seduction *by Cathy Williams*
Lorenzo wanted revenge. Isobel had betrayed
him once—now she had to pay. But the tears
and pain of sacrifice had been price enough.
Now she wanted to win him back.

FREE!

2 Books
and a surprise gift!

We would like to take this opportunity to thank you for reading this Mills & Boon® book by offering you the chance to take TWO more specially selected titles from the Enchanted™ series absolutely FREE! We're also making this offer to introduce you to the benefits of the Reader Service™—

- ★ FREE home delivery
- ★ FREE gifts and competitions
- ★ FREE monthly Newsletter
- ★ Books available before they're in the shops
- ★ Exclusive Reader Service discounts

Accepting these FREE books and gift places you under no obligation to buy; you may cancel at any time, even after receiving your free shipment. Simply complete your details below and return the entire page to the address below. ***You don't even need a stamp!***

YES! Please send me 2 free Enchanted books and a surprise gift. I understand that unless you hear from me, I will receive 4 superb new titles every month for just £2.40 each, postage and packing free. I am under no obligation to purchase any books and may cancel my subscription at any time. The free books and gift will be mine to keep in any case.

NOEB

Ms/Mrs/Miss/Mr ....Initials.................................
BLOCK CAPITALS PLEASE

Surname...

Address...

....

....Postcode ....

Send this whole page to:
UK: The Reader Service, FREEPOST CN81, Croydon, CR9 3WZ
EIRE: The Reader Service, PO Box 4546, Kilcock, County Kildare (stamp required)